Table of Contents

To Neomi and Tristan Kellum. I will always thrive to be better for you.

To Mike Rucker, the best friend I've ever known.

SECRET BAR

K. Banning Kellum

We all just want to be part of the inner-circle.

Every city claims to have them, and every city will tell you that theirs is the best. Larger places will lay claim to having quite a few. I am of course speaking of secret bars, or, in some cases, secret clubs. They generally fall under a simple concept. A bar with no name out front, where a secret password is required to get in. This is what started my obsession, and may have cost me my soul.

The year was 2001. I had turned 21 earlier that year and had already done up all the new freedoms that come with that age. I had done bars, strip clubs, casinos... you name it. At first it was so cool, because for years I had felt like a kid, like some wet behind the ears idiot that the rest of the world sort of just patted on the head. Even after turning 21, things remained annoying. People would hear that I was 21 and treat me not like an adult, but as a new adult, like a grown-up that still needed grown-ups. I was annoyed. I worked downtown in a dreary office job, inputting data. The nice thing about it though were my hours, 3pm to 11pm. For a single guy in his early 20s, it was perfect. I got to sleep in every day, and I would get off of work just in time to take the quick walk from the New Orleans Central Business District, cross over Canal Street, and bam, I was in the French

Quarter, land of booze and women. Lots of fun times were spent down there.

But as I said, even that began to get boring. Really boring. So, I began to research "secret bars." I found a few right away, and most of them were just as boring as the regular bars. One in particular, called Mythique, was located up a narrow stairwell, accessible only through a tiny door located under the bar downstairs. Once I got up there though, it was just another bar. The clientele was a bit more pretentious; most of them thought they were the second coming of Lestat, but in the end, it was the same thing—a bar, drinks, people and usually crappy music. I remember one night I was at home in my tiny apartment, using MetaCrawler (remember, this was 2001) and searching for more secrets in my city that I was now old enough to exploit. I kept finding links to the same boring places I always went to. Then my email binged, or I should say, announced, "You've Got Mail!"

I clicked open my email and saw the heading for the message read "Secret Bar." Now, I was sure if I had asked anyone on my AOL buddy list for help, and I didn't recognize the sender. I figured maybe I was in a chat room one night and asked around, but I figured it was worth a check. The email was simple and short and read something like this...

SECRET NEW ORLEANS BAR: Looking for a journey, not afraid of hell, not too shy for heaven, then come visit us. Be in Jackson Square tonight at 2am. Wear a black shirt and grey pants and have a cup of coffee in your hand. Seat yourself in the 3rd bench. This is your only invitation, miss it and you will never be invited again. PS: Come alone, tell no one.

That was the end of the email. I was lucky that my job required me to wear a suit because it just so happened that I had a pair of grey slacks. I pulled on a black t-shirt and realized that I actually looked pretty good. I figured this could be a prank, but even if it was, even it if turned out to be nothing, I would go out and have a few drinks anyway, maybe even get laid. I didn't have to go into work the next day, so tonight could turn out to be fun, anyway. However, I may have been a bored, idiotic 21-year-old, but I wasn't totally stupid. This could also be a trick, a trap or something worse. So, I called my best friend Mike up. I told him that I was going out with some strangers from work, and that I wasn't sure about them. I told him I would call him by 4am, and if I didn't, for him to call and check up on me. I told him I would be in the Quarter. Mike had to be up for work at 4am, so it wouldn't put him out of his way to call me when he got up.

I left my apartment at around 1:30am. I only lived about 15 minutes from downtown, but I figured I would make sure I was on time. By 1:55am I was sitting on the third bench in Jackson Square, sipping my coffee, and waiting.

At 2am, the Cathedral bells rang out twice, and I received a tap on the shoulder. A gorgeous woman was sitting next to me, and I thought to myself... this is too cliché to be real. To me, she seemed like a walking cliché for a "hidden bar." Goth girl, mid 20s, really hot... yeah, she was from the bar, I knew it from the start.

"I'm Jodie," said the woman.

"Well, at least you're not 'Raven' or 'Death' or 'Lilith' or some other stereotypical goth name," I replied, but I did so with a smile.

She returned my smile with one of her own. "Nope, always been Jodie, and you must be Kurt, right?"

She knew my name... very cool. Of course, my name was on my AOL profile where the email was sent, so if this was her attempt at a cool trick, I was one step ahead.

"Yes, Kurt, that's me. I guess you're here to show me to the secret bar?"

"Only if you're ready to journey to hell, or heaven... depending on your tastes. We like to consider this to be the first 'back out' point for new clients. You can decline the invitation now, and go home, or to some other bar, or wherever you'd like. Only be warned that no other invitation will ever come to you again."

I considered this, and decided that it was already after 2am, I was out, dressed and full of coffee. I wanted to see this place.

"Lead on, Miss Jodie!"

She stood up and began to walk ahead of me—at a rapid pace, I might add.

We walked in silence for some time, weaving deep into the Quarter, past Bourbon Street, past all the loud and drunk tourists, past the warm and safe lights, the cop cars, the music from the bars. Before long, we were in the dark part of the Quarter, mostly residential, and very few people were on the streets this way. She suddenly stopped and walked up the stoop to a private residence. She fiddled with keys, opened the door, and gestured for me to enter.

"Wait, is this someone's house?" I asked.

"This is the house where the dead scream in silence, where the walls rot, where pain becomes pleasure, where pleasure becomes death. This is the House of Din, He who dwells on the black star. Enter."

I thought this was the coolest pitch for a bar I had ever heard. I figured it was rehearsed, but she said that whole little phrase with a lot of conviction. I had no idea who Din was, and I certainly didn't know about black stars, but I did have a desire to push on.

She walked me into the house which was empty. No furniture, no nothing. Now, French Quarter real estate isn't cheap, so if this place was renting a house, just to serve as the cover for a bar, they clearly took themselves seriously. This might not be so boring after all.

What happened next was strange. She turned me towards a small hallway with an elevator. Now, I know that some houses back in the day had elevators. However, this one only appeared to go down. New Orleans isn't exactly known for having basements, especially in homes. As I went to step in, she stopped me once more.

"This is your second 'back out' chance. Same as before, you can turn around and leave, no harm, no foul."

"Push the button," I replied, pointing at the down button, and stepped in.

The elevator ride felt long, really long. At first, I was thinking that this was impossible, no one builds down in this city; hell, we even have to bury our dead above the ground. As far as I could see, though, we were going down. This was one of those older elevators with just the metal grate door. I could see wood and metal going past us, and this eventually gave way to stone. I was about to question this when it occurred to me...

"Cool trick," I said.

"Trick?" Jodie asked.

"Yeah, the elevator is rumbling in place while a rolling graphic goes by outside to look like we're going down, right? Because, while I am no expert on elevators, I would say that we'd have to be at least 20 stories below the city right now, and I know that just isn't possible."

"You're right," she replied, grinning. "We aren't 20 stories below the city. We are, by now, at least 2000 stories below, if you are using 'stories' as a measurement."

I wanted to say something back, about how that was a lie, had to be a lie, we hadn't been riding that long, and that amount of depth wasn't possible on a tiny elevator like this. However, I figured this was all part of the act, like her whole speech about the "House of Din" and all that crap. I didn't want to become too obnoxious or pushy. She might end up asking me to leave, figuring I would ruin the scene for other patrons. Instead I just smiled and decided to play along with a really cool and elaborate bar scene. Fake or not, this was by far the most ambitious effort I had ever seen put forward for a drinking establishment.

Shortly after, the elevator stopped. Jodie stepped in front of the doors, but before she opened them up, she turned back to me. "This is your final chance to back out. If you wish, I will take you back. However, once I open these doors, you will be in hell. You may find your way back to the surface tonight, but some find that leaving is just impossible. Some stay forever. In the interest of free will and fair play, I am bound by the Council of Nod to offer you this final chance to return to your life. Choose now."

"Amazing speech Jodie, really great, you guys clearly put some thought into this. Yes, I want to go to this bar."

She smiled and opened the doors. A small door sat at the end of a wooden hallway that looked like it may have been built around the time of the pyramids. There were no lights, I could only see by the small electric light in the elevator, and the light coming from the door ahead. I walked forward, and as soon as I stepped off of the elevator, the heat hit me. It wasn't so hot that I couldn't take it, but if anyone has ever experienced being in an attic on a really hot day, with no ventilation, then you'll have an idea of how this felt. The air was thick beyond description. I instantly was covered in sweat, and I knew that if I stayed in this hallway for too long, I would pass out. I turned to look back and saw the elevator already heading back up. From what I could see, there was no button to call it back down either. I guess Jodie wasn't kidding when she said that was my last chance to back out. I crossed my fingers that the bar would be air conditioned, and walked forward, into the light.

I entered that bar. It was small, very small, about the size of a bedroom. There was a single wooden bar, 3 bar stools pushed up to it, and 3 small tables in the corner area. The room was poorly lit; only a small light bulb, hanging from the cord, was providing the light. However, it was well-lit enough to see everything, and sitting right on the bulb seemed the most logical. There was a small shelf behind the bar, typical set up, liquor bottles in front of a mirror. There were 5 others in this room, plus the bartender. I saw a Gothic girl sitting at one of the tables, sipping a drink with a rather plain dressed man. There were two gentlemen at the other table. One was wearing a business suit, the other was wearing that awful 'cowboy' attire that was popular in almost all walks of life, even secret bars. There was another woman, average in appearance, probably in her mid 30s, smoking at the other side of the bar. Of course there was me too so that completed our little circle. There was no music playing. The walls were old wood, oak maybe. The bartender, now he was a classic. White shirt, black pants, suspenders and bow tie. Like something out of the roaring 20s. It was still hot too. Not as bad as the hallway, but pretty awful. Liquor would only make me hotter, but I was here now. I figured I would test the waters.

Now, as for liquor, I saw no bottles that I could recognize. None were labeled. There was no beer either. No name brands. No cash register. No bar mat. This place was as simple as you could want. After a moment, the bartender spoke to me.

"Welcome to Hell!" he announced, smiling.

"Cool name, sort of expected it, though." I tried not to sound rude or pretentious. They had put on a great show tonight, but calling the place Hell... really? Too predictable.

"Well, it translates differently in lots of places. Hell is just the way you know it. Shall I call it something else?"

"No, Hell is fine, how about a drink... Jack and Coke please."

"No Jack here, and no Coke either."

"What do you have then?"

"Well, most people down here have a drink we call Regret. I can also serve you Loneliness. Or if you're feeling particularly bold, our house special is Damnation."

"Wow, you guys are really playing up the hell thing. Okay, serve me some Regret please."

He handed me a drink poured from a brown bottle. It tasted amazing too. I figured it to be a bourbon and wished I had some Coke to mix it with. Apparently there was no ice here... I chuckled, of course not, ice in hell... what am I thinking? The drink was tasty though, and the buzz hit me quick.

I ordered up a Loneliness and begin to look around at my fellow patrons. None of them seemed to even notice me. The goth girl was cute though, so I picked up my drink and decided to walk over to her, when suddenly the woman sitting at the bar began to whimper.

"I am so thirsty... can I please have some water," she seemed to be pleading this to the bartender.

"No ma'am!" He replied with that same stupid grin. "No water in Hell, not even a small amount. Have another cigarette though. Wash it down with some hard liquor."

"No more smoking... my mouth is too dry... no more liquor... water please," she continued, and to me, it began to sound a lot like begging.

Instead of handing her water, he held out an unlit cigarette. It was then that I noticed the overflowing ashtray, the size of a damned punch bowl, sitting next to her. It was full of butts, had to be over a thousand of them in there. Had she smoked them all herself? I strained my eyes and studied her harder. He lips were blistered badly. She had been at it for a while. The bartender patiently held out the cigarette, the grin never leaving his face, until she finally sighed and took it. He produced a lighter, and she took a drag. She began to cough violently, gagging too. I decided to chime in.

"Hey man, she doesn't look so hot, and I really don't think she needs another smoke. She looks like she dying of thirst too. Call the elevator, man. She's had enough I think."

The bartender turned his big smile on me. "Who? Ol' Nancy here? Naw, Nancy is a trooper, man—smokes a couple packs a day. And as far as her thirst, well, she knew this place was a thirsty sort of dive before she walked in the door, but she wanted to be here. She is getting exactly what she wanted."

I walked over to Nancy and placed my hand on her shoulder. "Ma'am, if you want to get out of here, I'll walk you over to the elevator. You don't look so great right now." I tried to sound as concerned as a 21-year-old kid could sound.

Nancy looked at me and smiled. "Oh, I'm fine... just fine," she said, but her mouth quivered as she spoke.

The bartender was watching us like a hawk, still smiling, but his smile no longer looked so friendly. "Everything okay?"

Nancy shakily replied yes. The bartender turned around, and in that second Nancy gripped my arm hard, pulled me into the smog that was her breath, and whispered...

"Leave while you can," so low that I almost missed it. Her breath was like a chimney, she must have been chain smoking for days. I smoked, and so do most of my friends, and even on nights when we would chain smoke and pound booze until the sun rose, none of us were ever that toxic.

I walked over to the man in the business suit. He at least appeared sane.

"Hey sir, I think that lady over there needs help," I said to him.

The man looked at me and laughed. "We all need help, kid. We're in Hell after all!" he shouted.

As he did this, I looked over at the goth girl, just in time to see her begin to cut herself, deep and hard from the looks of it. The plain dressed man sitting next to her begin to laugh in a high pitched tone, almost a giggle, and that was when I noticed that he was masturbating. Only, not in the sense that we all do, at home. No, his penis was raw, bloody, torn away in places, but he just kept going at it.

"Stop that! Look at what you're doing to yourselves!" I screamed at them. They looked at me and I noticed that the girl was crying, but also smiling. Her eyes were practically begging to her self-inflicted pain to stop, yet she just kept cutting.

I had seen enough. I reached over and attempted to pull the knife out of her hand. Just then, I felt a strong grip on my shoulder, stronger than anything I had ever felt in my life. It was the bartender; he had come around the bar to grab me.

"No, NO sir!" he screamed into my ear. "Every patron of Hell gets to enjoy their treats without judgment. After all, judgment has already been passed. We exist beyond that now. Let her cut, she loves it after all, can't you see she loves it, she is smiling ear to ear!"

The bartender dragged me back to my stool, and with great speed, was somehow back behind the bar again.

"Now, you wanted secrets, right, Kurt? You were bored and wanted more. That is what you came for. Now drink your drink before I beat your fucking face in!"

Through all of this, he never stopped smiling. He slammed a glass before me. I murky liquid was inside. He grabbed my arm and begin to squeeze, the pain becoming unbearable. My mind began to race...this was no bar—this was something, but not a bar. I wasn't ready to believe I was actually in hell, but I knew I was somewhere bad.

"DRINK YOUR DRINK SIR!" he screamed again, and fearing that I would pass out from the pain, I slammed down the liquid in front of me. It tasted horrible. I couldn't describe it then, and I can't now, but it was fierce.

He let go of me, and suddenly the room got much hotter. The light began to flicker, and suddenly I was afflicted by knowledge. Things I didn't want to know, things that no one would want to know.

My mother had an affair... and the man I had grown up calling dad was in fact not my father at all.
I had a brother who died. I never knew that.

My boss at work hated me.
My grandfather committed suicide... all these years I just thought he died naturally.
My mother was going to abort me... but changed her mind because she couldn't afford the abortion.
I was going to die alone.
My wife, a woman I would meet in six years and fall madly in love with, would die in a car crash with my three-year-old son in the back seat. There was nothing I could do to change this.
I would go blind in my 60s from a work related accident.
There were currently 34 people in the world right now, some who I thought of as friends, who wanted me to die. They hated me.
No one, not my mother, not my father... no one had ever loved me, at all.

Those were just a few of the secrets that suddenly hit me. There were thousands, maybe millions more, but by then my mind couldn't process them all. There were some things, things about me, things about people I knew, that were so dark that I am thankful that I cannot remember them, because to dwell on them for even a second longer would have brought on madness.

Frantically I looked around the bar. The woman, Nancy, was still smoking, only her throat was on fire... a small red glow, smoldering, right in the middle of her throat. She was clearly in the worst pain of her existence, but she continued to take puff after puff of her cigarette. Each time she did, the glow on her throat would get brighter.

I looked straight ahead into the mirror behind the bar, seeing the gore fest that had begun behind me. However, what took my attention was the small, black figure, standing directly to my right. It was maybe 5 feet tall. Its skin was jet black. The only thing that stood out was its eyes. They were human eyes, but bright. Not glowing, just... bright enough to stand out from the onyx of its face. It had small horns on its head. It had very white, very sharp teeth.

Somehow, I knew this was Din, and I was in his house.

I looked towards the door, but it was gone. The heat continued to get worse. The secrets were still popping into my mind, each worse than the one before. Entire dimensions of my soul were being revealed to me. All of it horrible.

Just then, my cell phone rang. The ring tone, something from my world, something from up above. It grabbed my attention, and in that moment, the secrets slowed down a bit. I looked down, it was 4am... Mike, Mike was calling to check up on me.

His name, Mike... yes, I have a friend named Mike... my best friend. The more I focused on things that were real, the more stable things became around me. The secrets were almost stopping now. The macabre scene around me was slowing down too. Nancy was back to just smoking again. The goth girl wasn't cutting. That sinister face of Din... it had also retreated just a bit.

MIKE... MIKE... my oldest friend... yes, we grew up together, we rode our bikes together, we had sleepovers, pizza parties... and the more I focused on the real world... if I could just...

The door was back. I bolted for it.

"Stop! You had your chance to back out!" screamed the bartender, and I looked back just in time to see him leap over the bar behind me.

I shot through the doors and back into the tiny, impossibly hot hallway. The bartender burst through the doors, and I did the only thing I could think of. If thinking about the real world, weakened this place, then perhaps a real link to the real world would break it. I hit "answer" on my cell phone, and the voice of my best friend, who was calling from the safety of his apartment, greeted my ears. I could even hear music in the background, real music.

"Mike... call the cops, I am in real trouble here," I screamed into the phone.

"What, I can barely hear you man, your connection sucks."

The bartender was still coming, still grinning. I had one last idea.

I pushed "speaker."

Mike's voice, a product of the living world, owned by someone who had not made a deal to enter some level of hell, flooded the hallway. The bartender stopped.

"He is not allowed to know of this place... to have any contact without being invited... even voice contact... it violates the Council of Nod."

That was when the final blow to the bar from hell was delivered. I heard Mike, in his sleepy yet concerned voice, say, "What is the Council of Nod?"

Contact had been made. Whatever rules governed this place had been broken.

Suddenly, the elevator came down. The bartender, still smiling, looked down at me.

"Sorry, sir, but you have violated the rules. You are no longer welcome at this bar. Please leave."

Jodie was standing in the elevator. I stood up and climbed in. The effects of the drink I consumed were gone. No more secrets.

My phone had died; I guess calling from hell drains a battery. However, the effects were enough. We rode up in silence.

When we reached the surface, Jodie walked me out of the house, onto the stoop. Then she spoke. "You may think you won tonight, but you didn't. You had a chance to ride this elevator up as well as down. Your heart wanted secrets instead of happiness, though, so it went down. You could have gone up, and everything you could ever have possibly desired would have been yours. So, go on, feel proud. We like proud mortals because the proud ones always find their way back to Hell."

"Fuck you, Jodie," I replied, but did so as I was walking away. I didn't want to tempt these people anymore than I had.

When I got home that night, I remembered almost all the secrets. Over the years they have slipped away, slowly at first, then, like a dream, I would wake up and more would be lost. I wrote down the ones that I listed here because I didn't want to forget them all. However, when I read them now, they don't seem like secrets anymore, just like weird lies.

Of course, I called the police the very next day. I wanted to help those people down there. I had to dress up the story a bit. I told the cops that Jodie led me there after meeting her in the Quarter. I left out the part about the place possibly being a level of Hell and simply described it as a basement where people were being tortured. The cops got a warrant and went in. The house was empty as I said it was. However, there was no elevator found. The cops said there was a large closet area that appears to have had an old elevator at one time, but it was long gone now. The house itself was still on the market; it had no owner.

For a few years I would go down to Jackson Square around 2am, hoping to catch Jodie luring another victim into the house. However, I never saw her again. Years went on, I did marry, and no, my wife was never killed in a car accident. We don't have kids yet though. Perhaps when I violated the contract, the Council of Nod, or whatever, I somehow broke that cycle. I'll never know, but I will be careful. After I wrote down my encounter in the bar, I burned the list of secrets that I had scribbled down. Of course, I could always read them on here, but I won't. And in time, hopefully I will forget them too. I never confronted my mother about the abortion plan, or asked who my real dad was. Those secrets seemed so real, but Satan is also called the "Father of Lies" for a reason. I am not sure if Din is Satan or just a lesser version of him, but I doubt that Din is a very honest sort either.

I write this as a warning though, a warning to be careful when seeking out secrets. Some things are kept secret for a reason, and to know them is to know madness.

The Demon in the Mirror Trick

K. Banning Kellum

It's all fun and games until it smiles first.

This is an old trick, one I am sure many of you have tried. Dim the lights and stare into a mirror, letting your eyes go out of focus. Your face, the face you've known your entire life, will morph, twist and become demonic before your eyes.
This used to be a fun party trick, especially if you were telling a scary story while it was happening. Something about seeing your own face twist, it's unnerving in such a deep, personal way.

If you're reading this, just don't. I did recently, on the spur of the moment. I was walking out of my kitchen, and my bathroom door was open. There was just enough light from the kitchen to see the mirror. I stared forward as my face turn ugly; same as always... until the reflection smiled back.

I know little, but whatever is on the other side of the mirror hates me. Maybe because we view it as nothing more than our reflection, our property, something we used to comb our hair and brush our teeth. But it's alive... and full of hate.
I hear it at night, tapping on the mirror. It wants out. I tried to show my wife, but it's sharp. She simply sees the reflection, but as soon as she turns around, it grins at me.

The taps have become pounding. Not just at home anymore either. It goes wherever I go, and it wants me.

Tonight I am alone. The tapping has started... and now it's pounding. Its face is that twisted face. I figured this out. That deformed face... that isn't from our eyes going blurry. No, that's the demon's true appearance..
Oh God!
I heard glass shatter.

Joe Montana Saves the Princess

K. Banning Kellum

We all just sort of know when it's our turn to be the Quarterback.

The day was cool, a perfect Connecticut autumn morning. Cool enough for a light jacket yet not so cold that one could become uncomfortable. The sky was a perfect blue portrait of beauty. The birds were singing. The wind joined in their song by gently puffing among the trees, rattling the few stubborn leaves that simply refused to fall quite yet.

A young man of only eighteen years stands alone on a small dirt path. This young man, Brian Lawrence to his family, Brian to his friends and Big Bri to his long deceased brother, was dressed today in his usual attire. An expensive polo shirt tucked into a rather snazzy pair of slacks, a respectable pair of loafers on his feet, and a pair of sunglasses that cost more than most people spend on food in a month. To a random passerby, Brian was another product of the American success story, two wealthy parents, a good home on a wealthy piece of Connecticut estate and lots of friends.

Brian was even all set for college, finishing school with a promising GPA. A scholarship was already secured, partly by Brian's efforts, mostly by his father's connections. Either way, Brian was a young man on his way to the top. His father swore that in ten years Brian would be running a company somewhere, making big advances, shaking and moving, and most of all, keeping the untarnished Lawrence name on top.

So, maybe untarnished isn't the right word for the Lawrence family exactly. Even the most beautiful of faces often have a blemish or two, nothing that a quick pat down of makeup can't fix of course. Well, the Lawrence family had a blemish as well. As mentioned above,

Brian used to have a brother, Joseph.

Brian and Joseph were about ten years apart in age. However, this didn't seem to stop them from being the best of friends. Since the father of the Lawrence tribe was so often at meetings or work retreats, it fell on Joseph to be big brother and dad, something that he was more than happy to do.

Even now, as Brian stands on this dirt road, staring towards the enormous building in front of him, he reflects back on his times with Joe. After all, Joe is why he is here right now.

Brian thinks back to the best times he and Joe spent together. Those times of course, their almost nightly games of football played between the two brothers in their gorgeous back yard. This was almost a decade ago though. Back when Brian himself was only eight years old, and Joe himself was eighteen. Joe was on his way to college himself, and this was to be one of his last weekends at home.

Joe always pretended to be Joe Montana, and would usually appoint Brian to be either Jerry Rice or Roger Craig, depending on whether he was going to pass or run. Brian used to beg to be Montana, but Joe would typically laugh and tell him that he wasn't ready to be a Quarterback.

Brian remembered that weekend for far more than simply a game of backyard football though. That was also the week that

Joseph would be found murdered, his body left in the bushes of the park where he was jogging. The police would search and investigate; however, they would get nowhere. Months would turn into years, and finally those years would become a decade. Brian's parents would move on. Careers and such would demand it. Brian would spend the next decade going through the motions; achieving high grades, dating girls, being popular and beloved by both his friends and even much of the staff.

However, Brian knew something, something that he had held inside for years. He fully believed that he had the identity who killed Joseph, which is what lead him to this point, far away from the safety of Greenwich. Brian looked towards the end of the road, towards the Foundation of Christly Fellowship, or the Foundation, as it was known around town. Why was he here? His family didn't attend church here, nor did anyone he knew. So why did Brian come to the Foundation on this beautiful, crisp morning?

Honestly, even young Brian might have a hard time answering that question. Was he here for revenge? Was he here to expose the truth? Brian honestly didn't know. However, he knew that he had to make the nightmares stop, and he was almost certain that this was the place to accomplish that.

The Foundation was a huge building that sat on several acres of land in the woods west of Greenwich. It had been there forever, and Brian grew up hearing ghost stories about it all the time. Just the appearance of the building alone was enough to spark any number of scary stories, especially among kids. The main cathedral was in the front, and it alone was easily as tall as a five-story building. Built into the rear of the cathedral was the even more expansive abbey portion. This was a ghastly cube of a building, four stories tall with four spires on each end. The church was only accessible through a dirt road, and it even had its own graveyard around the back.

This place, just on appearance alone, was a gold mine of late night ghost stories. The rumors about the place just added fuel. Some kids said that devil worshippers held their Black Mass there on a regular basis. Others claimed to see all the windows flashing strange colored lights during the wee hours of the morning. One kid claimed that he once walked near the church at night and heard screams coming from inside.

Before Joe's death, Brian didn't buy into these stories much. They could be fun for a late night sleep over, but Brian wasn't impressed by the idea of an evil church. Come Joe's senior year, and his decision to go to college for journalism, he wanted to do a real story, something that would impress the high school administration that he was saying goodbye to, and also impress the college deans he would be saying hello to.

Joe chose to investigate The Foundation, spinning it as a famous hometown urban legend. Joe began asking around, going to shops and businesses that had been open in Greenwich for a long time. Most people that he talked to seemed to know very little. It was a secretive group that rarely exposed what they did. Membership was by invitation only. That was about all people would say about it.

Joe was actually considering dropping the story when he received a phone call one day from the Foundation itself. Joe had no idea how they got his home number as the Lawrence family was unlisted. The voice on the other end of the phone instructed Joe to let sleeping dogs lie and promptly hung up.

Joe had told Brian all about the creepy phone call, but Brian assumed Joe was just teasing him. Joe continued to ask his questions, and finally put together a fairly interesting article, although he was never able to see it published. Joe graduated high school shortly afterwards. A few months passed, and dead birds began to show up on the Lawrence yard every few mornings. Their father assumed it was kids. Joe had another idea.

He told Brian that he suspected he was being followed sometimes. He even found a flyer on his car, inviting him to come out to the Foundation for a special service. Joe said that he looked at all the other cars, and his was the only one with the invitation.

Brian was still convinced that Joe was just messing with him though. Finally came the fateful week. Joe had gone to the park for a morning jog and had simply never come home. That was when he was found murdered, his throat slit.

Joe was buried. The family mourned. Time went by and things began to return to normal. All of that changed when Brian began to have the nightmares.

For ten years he was visited nightly by visions of Joe's murder. In all of them, Brian was running through the park, looking for Joe. He would see Joe jogging and would call out to him. Before Joe could look though, a man in dark robes holding a jeweled dagger with a twisted blade would step out. Joe would try to stop running, but could never stop in time. The dagger would be plunged into his throat, and the robed man would begin to walk away.

Brian would chase him in these dreams, and in every single one, the robed man would lead Brian back to The Foundation. Brian would follow the man into the cathedral, only to hear the doors slam behind him. The robed man would be waiting for him, and would always say the same things.

"Your brother was charged with the sin of knowledge, and the Camiastra, our sacred blade, delivered to him the Judgment of the Gray Omen."

Brian would stand there, frozen, while the robed man would move towards him.

"Your brother is now in the ground, beneath our feet."

There would be a loud scream, like a woman shrieking in a rage, and a bright and brilliant light would fill the room. This is where Brian would awaken, shaking and covered in a cold sweat. This had been his life for the last ten years.

He told his parents about the nightmares. At first, they told him it was just normal, because he had just lost his brother. Later they would tell him that it was normal because of the stress of high school. Most recently, they told him it was normal because college was coming up.

Brian knew better though. He knew that no matter what sort of nightmares he was having, his parents would always say it was nothing to worry about. The only other option might be take Brian to therapy, and in the Lawrence family, such things just didn't happen. They were far more concerned with how such a thing might affect their reputation at the country club. As far as the Lawrence parents were concerned, one crisis was enough.

That brings us back to the present where Brian now prepares to step into the Foundation. He doesn't want to, but he knows that he must. These dreams have turned into obsessions. His logical mind tells him that what he'll find inside will be just normal people; normal church folks, folks that will probably be friendly and happy to talk to him. He hopes that if his mind can be put to ease, that this obsession with the Foundation will be put to rest along with it, thus ending these nightmares.

Brian approaches the doors, half expecting them to be locked. However, they open easily, despite their massive height, revealing the cathedral that until now had only been seen in his dreams.

He is taken back at how similar the actual inside is to his dream.

"Just a coincidence," he tells himself. "Seen one church, seen them all."

A crimson carpet runs the center of the church. Two rows of pews occupy either side. The stain glass windows appear to be images of Saints and other biblical figures. They all look down on Brian, all with disapproving expressions on their faces. The altar is at the end of the carpet. It is covered in a crimson cloth, much like the carpet.

He walks slowly down the center, sensing out of place here. His legs feel heavy. The carpet makes a gentle swish sound under his feet. Besides himself and the frowning Saints on the windows, he is alone. He walks to the altar and looks upon it. Four candles sit at each corner. A black ring of fabric is the only detail in the otherwise solid red cloth.

"Guess they lock up the expensive stuff when service isn't going on."

In his determination to explore the cathedral, he never notices that large oak doors slowly close.

Brian pokes around a bit more, finding nothing of interest. He decides that this was a waste of time. No one is here.

"They must leave the doors unlocked for people to come in and pray."

He turns to walk back to the exit and notices the doors are now shut. Thinking that it was just the wind, he begins to walk towards them. Upon arrival though, he finds them both to be locked.

"Oh shit... the damned things closed and locked," he whispers.

Still grounded in reality, Brian is not particularly concerned about this. Worst-case scenario, he tells someone that he wandered in to use the phone or whatever, and became locked in. What were they going to do, call the Jesus Police on him?

Brian scans the room and sees a small door to the left of the altar.

"That must lead into the abbey. I'll just find the priest and ask to use the phone."

A dark thought briefly crosses Brian's mind though. They had called Joe on the phone, told him to back off. Brian shivered a bit at this thought.

"Stay calm... that's what Joe would say right now. When he used to throw me the long passes, he would say... stay calm Jerry Rice, stay calm and keep your eye on the ball... so, the ball is me getting out of here, so, let me just get my eyes on that."

Brian walked towards the small wooden door when he suddenly felt a chill. He was being watched, or at least had that sensation. He darted his eyes in the direction of the sensation and noticed that he was standing underneath an air vent. For just a moment, a split second, he thought he saw a face staring at him from inside the vent, and then it was gone.

"C'mon Jerry Rice, stay calm."

Brian turned the old metal knob on the door and was amazed when it opened. He was sure that it would have been locked. Now he just had to find someone.

The door opened into a long set of dark oak halls. The halls were lined with doors on either side. He began to walk down the hall, hoping to find an office or a rectory room. This place seemed like it would go on forever.

He reached an intersection and went to the right, leading to a stairwell. Not a normal one either, but one of those old winding stairwells. He thought about going back and trying the left hall, but the stairs were here and being lost going up was no different than being lost going to the left. He ascended the spiral stairs, coming out on the second floor landing.

"Okay, this looks good," he thought to himself as he saw the next floor.

It looked like where the living quarters would be. The floor was carpeted, and there were comfortable looking benches along the walls. He felt hopeful that this would lead him to a friendly nun, or maybe even the stereotypical Irish priest.

He walked on and noticed that there were framed plaques along the wall. He paused to read on.
The interloper is the greatest foe of the Un. None pose so great a threat to the Birth of the Un than the interloper.

Below that bizarre little quote was a woodcarving styled image of a man peering through a keyhole.

Brian pondered on the strange message.

He walked a bit further and found another plaque.
The Birth of Un will mark the Grand Occurrence, so set in motion by our first brothers. When the bloodline of Tier should make itself known, we shall have their daughters unto Un.

Brian was becoming more convinced that perhaps this place was some sort of outlandish cult.

He kept telling himself that they wouldn't be dangerous... they would help him. Just because their beliefs were exotic, that didn't make them evil, or so he hoped.

The final plaque read:
He of the House Tier, whom in his Unholy rescue of the Traitor St. Simon, whom did prevent the First Occurrence, shall pay for his sin with the blood of his daughters. In in the wash of this daughter's blood, the stain of Tier shall be washed away, and Un will be brought forth, ushering in the Grand Occurrence, and the glory of the Gray Omen.

With that, Brian's heart froze. In that moment, all the nightmares suddenly became real. The Gray Omen, the name whispered to him in his countless dreams, countless dreams in which his brother was murdered before his eye, was suddenly before him, in the world of the waking.

Brian came and got what he was looking for. There was the link, and it wasn't a friendly nun or an Irish priest. This plaque may not prove that this church killed Joe, but it certainly lent a strong lead that they were involved. It also lent heavy validation to his dreams.

That's when he heard voices coming down the hallway. Two men. He couldn't hear exactly what they were saying, but he knew by the rise of their voices that they were coming in his direction. At that moment, Brian no longer wanted to ask them for help. He would find his own way out of here. After all, the plaque itself clearly states that interlopers are frowned upon here. Brian wasn't interested in finding out if they would believe that he was simply lost and looking for a phone.

Peering quickly around the halls, he spotted an alcove a few meters ahead and to his right. Without thought, he ran into the alcove, and took cover underneath a bench. The voices of the two men were not close enough to make out.

"So the girl is still running loose in here, and now we have another one."

"Yes, however, Father Haller sensed his coming for some time. It would appear he finally came forth."

"Do you think he will interfere?"

"No. The stars will be aligned correctly tonight for the first time in almost two-thousand years. We are pretty sure we can flush the girl out. She can't hide forever, especially without food. As for the boy, he is not important. Once the Grand Occurrence is complete, we won't even have to concern ourselves with the likes of trespassers."

"They know I'm here... they're hunting for me right now..." Brian's mind raced.

He could now see their legs as they stopped to chat, right next to the alcove. Brian began frantically searching for a way out.

The slight brisk, warm air that hit his face caught his attention. A vent. The grate outside of the vent was large, large enough for him to crawl into, perhaps. He didn't have time to think it over. He was a strapping boy of almost six feet. He knew this bench wouldn't conceal him for long.

The grate was designed to swing in and out. As quietly as possible, Brian pushed in the grate, and began to slide himself into the vent shaft. It was in fact large enough to accommodate him.

Slowly, and as carefully as a surgeon making the first cut, Brian crawled into the vent. Everything was going well for him at first, pulling his body in was easy. The inside of the vent was spacious enough. He thought he was in the clear, until he felt a painful clamp on his left foot, and he could pull himself no further.

The grate had fallen closed on his foot. Brian tried to pull forward anyway, but it was caught around his ankle in just the right way. Pulling only brought on shooting pains. He tried to use his other foot to free himself, but the grate had to open inward, and try as he might, he couldn't hook his foot under enough to lift the grate up.

His only hope now was to contort his body around and lift the grate by hand. He could still hear the voices of the two men outside as well; they hadn't left. Worse, it sounded like one of them had sat down on the small bench. It would only be a matter of time before one of them looked down long enough to notice a brown loafer sticking out of their air vent. Then it would be all over.

Brian twisted around as best he could, using all the space available, reaching for the grate. He focused all his will, all his strength or reaching it. Still, he was at least a foot away. The walls of the vent would not permit him to inch any closer. As he tried to pull his arm back, his elbow struck the wall of the vent.

"What was that?" he heard one of the men say.

"Sounds like something in the walls, could be the girl."

Brian knew he was almost out of time. With one last lunge, he reached again for the grate, but still came up a foot short. He closed his eyes and strained. Suddenly he was in his backyard again on was a warm night; fireflies dotting the darkening sky.

"Heads up, Jerry Rice!" shouted the familiar voice of Joe.

Brian looked up just in time to avoid getting struck in the face by a whirling football.

"Whoa Jerry, you almost lost your head there."

Brian picked up the football and threw it back to Joe.

The throw was a bit short, landing on the ground about ten feet in front of his brother.

"See, that's why you're not ready to be Joe Montana!" laughed Joseph.

Brian was relieved. He had a thought in the back of his mind that something bad had happened to him, but perhaps it was just a dream. Here was Joe, alive and well, throwing the ball just like always.

Joseph ran over to Brian, the football in hand.

"Okay Big Bri, let's try that pass again. You were so close."

"Sure," Brian answered.

Joe ran out to the middle of their backyard and launched the ball hard. Brian ran backwards, trying to keep up with it so he could dive and make the catch.

"Brian, go for it, you are so close," called Joe.

Brian ran, extending his arm as far as he could.

"Brian, you have to stretch, you have to reach. REACH for it Brian."

The ball was coming down; still it looked like it might be just a bit out of Brian's reach.

"Brian, you can do this, you're so close. You have to reach for it. Time is running out on the clock."

Brian dove to the ground, stretching his arm as far as he could. The ball landed in his hand. He smiled.

Except, it didn't feel like a football. It was cold, and hard, metallic. Brian opened his eyes.

He was in the air vent... still in the church. Everything was the same. Except now his hand was firmly touching the air grate. How? He didn't take the time to ponder that here and now, he lifted the grate and pulled his foot in. He crawled forward, deeper into the darkness, just in time to hear the bench slide over.

"I can't see anything in there," said one of the men from out in the hallway.

"I'll go get a flashlight," responded the other.

Brian didn't want to wait around for them to come back with essentials. He continued to crawl forward, eventually turning a corner.

From behind him, he heard one of the men, in a mocking voice, call, "If you're in there, we'll find you. You're not going home today, kiddo."

Brian crawled on for a bit. Every time he came across another grate, he would hear voices in the hallway. It was either the two men from before, or someone just as bad. He kept hoping to find a vent shaft that would take him back to the main cathedral.

Suddenly he heard the base of the shaft that he was crawling through begin to moan under his pressure. He froze. His heart pounded. After a moment of stilled panic, when nothing happened, Brian placed his hand out in front of him to crawl further.

In the next second the shaft gave out and Brian found himself falling.

Brian hit the floor in the room below with a painful thud. Stars danced before his eyes. After a moment of regaining his composure, he realized that he had landed in a study of sorts.

It was a small room, with books lining either wall. A small sofa and a couch were present, and he damned his luck for managing to miss both of them when he fell from the ceiling.

Brian steadied himself to his feet. Within seconds he heard movement on the other side of the study door. He froze again. He heard the jingle of keys.

Still frozen, Brian had no time to search for a place to hide. He was caught. He had no hope. He heard the door unlock. He watched the doorknob begin to turn, and he braced himself for whatever fate awaited him.

The door opened. Before Brian was not the harbinger of death that he had expected, but rather a beautiful young woman, of perhaps eighteen or nineteen years of age. To Brian, she looked almost like an angel; her most noticeable feature being her hair, which was a solid white. Her eyes were of the deepest blue he had ever seen. In that moment, he actually could have believed that she was an angel from heaven.

"We have to hurry, I know a safe place," said the girl.

"Who are you... who are these people...?"

"No time to explain here, I am sure they heard you crash through the ceiling. We have to go!"

Brian didn't know who she was or why he should trust her, but she had to be better than whatever else might be hunting him at the moment.

He followed her through a series of hallways. She seemed to have a set of keys and was amazingly able to pick the correct key each time. She moved with a speed and grace that Brian found almost unnatural.

Finally they turned into a small room, and she locked the door behind them. It appeared to be a pantry. She took a bottle of water for herself from the shelf and handed one to Brian. He drank greedily. All this time he didn't realize just how dry his mouth had become.

"Okay," she said, after downing half a bottle.

For the next half an hour or so, the white haired woman who had come to be Brian's savior explained the bizarre circumstances that led to their meeting today. She began with Brian's very own entrance, something that she had been watching from an air duct much like the one he had fallen from.

"I saw you come in today. God only knows why you would choose to come here. This place is a death trap," she began.

"Honestly, I am not so sure why I came here myself. Now I just want to get out." She nodded at his statement as if that told her everything she needed to know.

"Why are you here?" he asked her.

"My name is Cindy Tierney. I am from Providence, Rhode Island. A few weeks ago, right around the time I was looking into colleges; my parents received a letter from this place. They convinced my parents that this place was a school, some sort of alternative college. Not only did they offer to pay for my education, but they also offered my parents a good deal of money if they would convince me to come to school here. So, being that we were not exactly wealthy to start with, they agreed and brought me here."

"The fact that it's a church didn't alert them that this might not be a school?" Brian asked.

"Like I said, they convinced my parents that this was some sort of alternative school. All they wanted to do was show me around, let me get a feel for it, at least, that's what they told my folks. When we got here, they showed us around a part of the building that could have passed as a school of sorts. They asked me if I would be willing to spend three nights here, to get an idea of the area. My parents... they were all for it. The guy that showed us around, he was a real charmer. Had them eating out of his hands. He offered to put my parents up in the best hotel in Greenwich. All expenses paid."

"And your parents went for it?" Brian interjected.

"Of course they did. They're good parents, but we are really broke. They weren't sure how I was even going to go to college, and then, like a miracle, this place calls us, offers to fly us out there for free. I am fairly sure my parents have never stayed in a Five-Star hotel with unlimited free room service. I think they were as excited about getting a mini-vacation as they were about me going to a free school. Like I said, the guy, Mr. Levit, he was a real charmer."

"So what happened?" he asked her.

"My parents left. Levit showed me to a room and told me that one of the school counselors would be around to explain how the program works. The first day was fine. I asked them why they chose me out of so many other more gifted kids. They told me that I was gifted in a unique way. I asked them what they meant, but all they would say was that it would be revealed.

"The second day is when things started to get strange. I asked to use the phone, so I could call my parents and let them know how things were going. That guy Levit told me that phone calls weren't permitted during the three day interest period. He told me that I needed to focus on preparing for the school. Keep in mind, no decision to attend their so called school had been made.

They still wouldn't give me a straight answer as to why they even wanted me. Finally, I demanded to call my parents. I told them I didn't care what their rules were that I wanted to speak with my parents."

"What happened then?" asked Brian.

"The guy Levit said, sorry Princess, no calls."

She continued, "At first I thought he was calling me "princess" in the sarcastic way, but I certainly wasn't acting like some spoiled rich girl, because I'm not. I got annoyed and asked him not to call me that. He replied by saying, why not, it's your title by birthright?"

"Of course I had no idea what he meant by that, but this place had begun to weird me out too much. There were no other kids here at all, and not once had anyone spoken to me about attending classes, what my major would be, nothing. Finally I demanded an answer."

"What did they tell you?" Brian inquired.

"They told me that I came from some kind of bloodline, the House of Tier. They said that some ancestor of mine had done something and that I was the only remaining daughter. That was too much for me to take. I told them I wanted to leave immediately and began to walk out. I would walk to town if I had to, but this place was too far out in the Twilight Zone for me.

"That's when they got aggressive. Levit grabbed me and threw me in my room. He told me that the Great Occurrence or something was happening tomorrow night, and that I would have to be in attendance."

"What did you do then?"

"I panicked. I screamed for help, and when I did, Levit flew up against the wall. He dropped his key ring. I just grabbed it and ran. That's when; well, when the usual stuff happened."

"Usual stuff?" asked Brian.

"Yeah, ever since I was a kid, I just sort of, knew what to do in certain situations. If bullies were chasing me, I always knew exactly where to run and hide. If I had a test that I didn't study for, my pencil seemed to just spell out the answers for me. I always figured I just had great luck. But yesterday, when Levit was chasing me, I just knew which doors to take. I knew which keys opened which doors, I don't know, that stuff just comes to me."

Brian spoke up, "That name, Tier, I read it on these plaques. Something about the Grand Occurrence, and the House of Tier. Is that why they wanted you here?"

"My last name is Tierney, I guess it could be related, but, why did he say I was a princess?"

"I have no idea, Cindy. These people are nuts though. The reason I came here today was, well, I think they killed my brother. After he died, I just kept having these nightmares, and the dreams always lead me here. It sort of became an obsession. I've been having these nightmares every night for a decade. I guess I was hoping that if I came here, saw this place, met some members, that I would realize they were just normal people."

“Why do you think they killed your brother?” asked Cindy.

Brian explained, telling the story of how Joe was going to do a story about the church. He told her about the cops finding Joe's body in the park, with his throat slit.

"The killer in the dreams always mentioned something about the Gray Omen. When I read those plaques today, there it was, right in front of me, in bold print.

"But the real question is, why are you still stuck in here. You say you have this… ability to find your way through stuff, why not use it to just, escape?"

Cindy frowned, which to Brian, made her appear even more beautiful.

"Every time I try to use the ability to find my way out of here, I just end up getting lost. It's fine for escaping inside of the building, but using it to get out, that's another thing."

Brian stood up and rubbed his chin. He knew it was time for him to take charge and get them both out of this church. After all, Brian himself had always been a quick success at all he tried. Sports, debate team, anything really. He wouldn't go so far as to claim that he had any powers, but he was a natural at most anything he tried. Plus, he was a Lawrence. When he did get out of this place, he was going to make sure his dad sued these sick bastards into the ground.

"Okay, maybe going out the front door isn't the answer. For a building this size, there has to be multiple exits." Brian presented this idea, still rubbing his chin, trying his best to remember the exterior of the building.

Cindy spoke up, "Well, when they were giving me and my parents a tour of the place, I remember that near the fake school area, there was a garden terrace. I've been afraid to wander this place alone, but now that you're here…"

She began to blush. Brian smiled at her, showing perfect teeth that years of regular cleanings and expensive whitening had given him.

“Do you think we can find it?”

“If I focus on the classroom, and not the exit, maybe my gift will kick in."

“Okay then, Cindy, you lead the way.”

They were on the move quickly. Cindy moved swiftly, always going for the right key without hesitation. At one point she turned and walked automatically into what Brian thought was a broom closet. When she opened the door though, it was just a small corridor that led down to the ground floor. She did this without breaking stride.

They came to a short flight of stairs going up, but they could both see sunlight not far up ahead.

“I’ll go first Cindy, just to make sure no one is waiting for us.”

Cindy smiled and squeezed Brian’s hand.

He climbed the stairs and came out in a small area that appeared to be an atrium complete with glass walls, a ceramic floor and pleasant looking furnishings. Brian walked a few feet in, saw no one, and turned back to call for Cindy. She appeared at the top of the stairs, but she had a look of utter misery on her face.

Behind her stood a blonde man in an expensive suit; he was all-smiles as he held a large knife to her throat.

Brian went to lunge forward, but felt a cold steel against the back of his head.

“No, no, no. Don’t move. Don’t move a fucking muscle!” ordered a male voice from behind him.

"The game has gone on long enough Cindy, we've spent a lot of time tracking you down, and the time for running and hiding is over," said the man with the knife to her throat.

"What do you bastards want with me!" shouted Cindy.

The man with the knife feigned a sad look, "Now, now, is that anyway for a princess to speak?"

"Why do you keep calling me that? Just who the hell are you?" she demanded.

"Why, we are the honorable servants of Un, the God-King. You are Princess Cynthia Tierney, last surviving daughter of the House of Tier; the very traitor that prevented the First Occurrence almost two thousand years ago. Such a shame how you kids don't know your family legacies anymore."

"Well, she's not exactly the last daughter, there is her mother," mocked the man standing behind Brian.

"Of course, the mother with ovarian cancer, the mother that will either die or be left barren. No, she's of no concern," answered the knife wielder.

"What...?" whimpered Cindy.

"Oh my, she didn't know. Cindy, why do you think your parents were so thrilled to accept our money and leave you here? Your mom is dying, and not slowly. She needs a surgery. When we learned of that little gem, we knew we had you right where we wanted you.

"You are the last daughter that could possible spawn more Children of Tier. Your blood, when given to sacrifice tonight, will wash clean the disaster of the First Occurrence, and will usher in the Grand Occurrence. Our God-King Un will rise, and we, his most loyal of servants, will be made masters of this world."

The man behind him forced Brian down into a kneeling position; he still felt the cold steel on the back of his head.

Suddenly, a voice spoke, directly into his left ear. A voice he knew immediately.

“Tough play you got here Big Bri.”

“Joe?” asked Brian, only to feel the steel dig harder into his skull as the gunman ordered him to shut up.

“Bri, speak to me in your mind, this is going to be a snap play, can’t let the opposing team know what’s coming.”

“Joe…” Brian spoke in his mind, “How are you here…?”

Brian heard the sarcastic laugh that his brother always saved for a question that he thought was silly. He could almost picture Joe’s crooked grin as let out that chuckle.

“Bri, this is no time to question your Quarterback. Now, I’ll be Joe Montana, as always, and you get to be Roger Craig this time around. This is going to be a running play alright.”

“What if he shoots me when I move?”

“Look, trust your QB kid. Now, here’s what you’re going to do.”

Cindy was staring ahead, the blade to her throat and regretting that Brian had to be in this situation. She intended to look over to him and mouth "I’m sorry" or some such sentiment. What she saw when she looked at him brought her amazement.

For one, he was smiling, and had a look of determination that certainly didn’t fit this particular situation. For two, his right leg was twitching. Three, he was staring directly at the man behind her, and for all she could tell; it looked like he was sizing him up.

The knife man, whose real name was Phillip Walker, never expected what came next. Walker had the knife, and his pal across from him had the gun. They had complete mastery of the situation. In fact, Walker was already preparing to receive praise from Father Haller when he turned the girl over. His mind was a million miles away from anything other than complete and total victory.

Then Brian darted.

He heard the gunfire, felt the heat off of the bullet as it came within inches of his face, but instead buried itself into the floor. Brian moved forward with a speed neither of the men was prepared for. He tucked his head and stuck out his shoulder, the simple charging tackle technique that Joe had taught him when he was a kid.

Cindy, understanding what was happening, pushed Walker's arm away and dove to the side, just as Brian rammed into Walker with all his might. Walker was aware of the young man striking into him, shoulder first. Walker was aware of falling backwards onto the stairs that he was standing in front of just moments ago. Walker was aware of his feet flying up while all the weight of his body suddenly rested on his neck. Walker was aware of a slight, barely audible popping sensation in his neck, and then Walker lost all awareness of everything.

"You little shit!" screamed the man with the gun. Brian got to his feet and turned around, just in time to see the gunman taking aim. That is when the second miracle occurred.

Cindy stepped forward, and with a shriek cried out.

"NOOO!"

Gunman suddenly felt as if a Mac truck had struck him. His back impacted the wall and his head snapped back and made a crunching noise. Gunman slowly slid to the floor and gave no more interference to either of the young people.

"Cindy... how did you...?" Brian gasped.

"Part of the gift I suppose. No princess should leave home without psychic screams!" She smiled, and Brian smiled back. For the first time today, things were looking up.

Brian picked up the gun, and both he and Cindy made their ways out onto the terrace.

"Okay, my car is about a quarter of a mile from here. I left it on the side of the highway right before the dirt road that leads here. I think if we move fast, we can get back to the city."

She nodded. Brian took her hand, which was cool and delicate, much like that of a princess, and began to lead her towards the road.

They were halfway down the dirt road when a man in lavish robes, purple, green and gold, stepped out in front of them.

"A merry chase. Good show Mr. Lawrence, but much like your brother, it is time for you to bow out," the man spoke. He looked to be in his sixties. Very fit looking for a man his age. His gray hair was combed back. He spoke with distinction.

Brian raised the gun at the man in front of him.

"Move or I shoot," he said, trying to sound convincing.

"Oh, I doubt that; a spoiled child like you? Why, had we not taken away your brother, you would be off on your daddy's yacht right now. You have certainly never committed a murder. Oh my no, people like you would never think of such a thing."

Brian cocked the hammer of the gun, "I'll do it... I will!"

"No, you won't. Not that it would make much of a difference to one like myself. Now, the game ends here."

Brian amazed himself when he felt his finger squeeze down on the trigger. The gun never fired though. Only a dry popping noise was heard.

Suddenly, the man was standing only inches from Brian, how he had moved so quickly was a thing of wonder.

Cindy screamed and held out her arms.

"BE GONE!" she bellowed.

The robed man didn't move. Instead he held out his own arm, and Brian was suddenly flying back through the air. He landed on the gravel road with a hard thud. He could hear Cindy screaming for help. He looked up and saw two more men emerge and grab her. Was the robed man somehow suppressing her abilities? Brian attempted to stand, but felt a heel of a booted foot come down on his head. His vision blurred, he felt another kick but barely registered it.

Then all went black.

Brian awoke, though he did not know how long he had been out. The first thing he saw was a red carpet. Slowly he lifted his head, which ached severely, and realized that he was back in The Foundation; the main cathedral to be exact. There were two large men standing on either side of him. He looked left and right quickly and realized that there were probably about two-dozen others in the large church. Their undivided attention focused towards the altar. It was there he saw Cindy, tied to a wooden beam.

The man in robes from the road entered from the main cathedral doors and slowly walked down the aisle. As he passed, members stood. When he passed Brian, the two men violently pulled him to his feet.

"Stand when Father Haller passes, you worm!" snarled one of the men.

Haller took center stage directly in front of his altar.

"My people, tonight we celebrate the Grand Occurrence. Two thousand years we have spent, correcting the actions of Traitor King Tier. Two thousand years since King Tier stopped the very first Agents of the Gray Omen from ending the life of the False Saint Simon. 2000 years we have spent working generation after generation, waiting for the night when the stars would align, and our God-King Un could once again be called forth to claim this world.

"Tonight, we have finally brought the last daughter of Tier, Cynthia Tierney, to justice. Tonight, her blood shall be spilled so that Un may once again live. Un, who governs over the Treasury of Hell, Un who shall reward us, his most faithful servants with eternal life, eternal wealth, and eternal power. We stand tonight on the first shore of a new continent. We stand tonight on the precipice of glory. With Princess Cynthia Tierney's blood, we begin this world again...

Now I prepare the Camiastra, our most Holy Instrument, for the ritual."

Haller removed a large, jeweled dagger from its case. He held it towards the congregation, who all gasped and moaned in ecstasy at its very sight. Brian recognized the blade at once. He had seen it in every dream he had for the last ten years. He knew, at that moment, that the blade in Haller's hands was the blade that took Joe's life.

Haller lowered the blade and began to slide it across Cindy's cheek. Her blood fell onto the altar. As the drops landed, a groaning sound, like steel and earth being shifted violently about, began to emit from below the church.

“Yes, YES! He is coming my people, HE IS COMING!” screamed Haller in glee.

He dragged the knife down Cindy’s arm, brings more blood, and suddenly, on the wall behind the altar, opened a vast, black hole. The wall crumbled, and Brian could hear something large, something primitive, breathing within that hole.

“Prepare yourselves my children, for now comes the death blow, and with that shall come Un, our King, our Savior, our path to Glory!”

Haller raised the Camiastra.

That was when Cindy’s eyes became a solid white, as white as her hair.

“Nooooooooo!!” she bellowed in such a voice, a voice that would make gods stop and notice. Her scream shattered the windows of the church. Father Haller was blown back, landing on the floor at the base of the altar.

With a force of pure energy, Cindy tore off the ropes that were binding her to the post. Her white hair was flowing above her head as though the very forces of the air were dedicated to her. Her body began to glow a bright white, just like her eyes. Her feet never touched the ground as she moved forward.

Some members of the congregation attempted to charge her. Cindy looked down towards them, a smile on her face, and with a flick of her wrist, sent them flying across the room. Other members must have decided that perhaps world domination wasn’t quite to their liking anymore, as they charged towards the doors, threw them open, and ran for their lives.

The two men that were holding Brian stepped towards Cindy, pulling guns from their jackets. They opened fire. She shifted her gaze in their direction, held out her hand and stopped the bullets in midair.

The two goons that fired the shots began to back up. Cindy flicked her wrist and the four bullets flew back, striking the men down.

"Brian, run, escape while you can!" Cindy called to him.

Brian began to back up towards the open cathedral doors. Suddenly, Haller reappeared, speaking in some unknown language. Cindy was knocked to the floor.

"Big Bri, looks like your girlfriend has gotten herself into quite a mess," spoke the voice of Joe, once again, directly into Brian's ear.

Now that Haller had regained some control, other cultists were beginning to move towards Cindy as well.

"Joe... I don't know what I can do," Brian said in a low voice.

"Well, how long do you think she can keep that up? Haller is going to outlast her. She is very powerful, but this guy has been in the game a long time. He knows how to hedge his bets."

"Tell me what to do Joe, please!" Brian begged.

"I can't. Not this time. I am all out of plays. It's time for you to be the Quarterback.

"Brian, it is time for you to be Joe Montana."

Brian's mind was hectic. His thoughts were going in all directions.

Cindy pushed out another burst of energy, forcing the group of cultists back. Haller seemed unaffected though.

"Be Montana," Brian heard in his mind. He wasn't sure if it was his voice, or Joe's. It didn't matter.

Brian looked towards the altar. Whatever was in that hole was waiting to come out. That's when he saw Haller's dagger, the Camiastra. He had dropped it when Cindy mind blasted him. Brian cleared his head. He pictured himself in his backyard again. Only now he was the big kid. Now he was Joe Montana. He began to speak to himself, low and determined, just like his brother spoke to him before they would execute one of their many plays.

"Okay, the Camiastra is the football. That black hole in the wall is the end zone. I am going to assume that Haller needs that knife to complete the ceremony. Get the knife and get the knife to the hole. Get the ball; get the ball to the end zone."

Brian sprinted forward. A cultist attempted to restrain him. Brian threw a punch and felt the satisfaction of the cultist's nose breaking. The man fell away with a groan. Haller, occupied with trying to restrain Cindy, had no time to react as Brian charged the altar, grabbed the Camiastra, and hurled it with all his might into the black hole in the wall.

"Oh you little fucker!" screamed Haller, taking his attention off of Cindy for the first time.

Haller reached forward and balled his fist. Brian suddenly fell to the ground. It felt as though his heart was in Haller's hand.

"You will pay for that boy! You will suffer in such a way that your brother's death will look like a blessing. You will scream until your throat breaks. You will...."

Haller's litany of threats was cut short. He had taken his attention off of Cindy for too long. Now he was being lifted off of the ground as the glowing white Princess stood behind him.

"You want your knife, then go get it!" she screamed, and Haller was thrown towards the hole. Haller threw out his arms and stopped just short of the hole in the wall. He turned back to face her.

"You still are not ready for the likes of me, you feeble little twit!" shouted Haller. With a thrust of his arms, Cindy was brought down to the ground, hard. Her glow began to fade. Haller began to walk towards her, stopping long enough to pick up a shard of broken stain glass from the floor.

"Perhaps the ritual will not be as proper without the Camiastra, but I think your blood will taste as fine to Un regardless of how it is spilled." Cindy was unable to crawl away. She has simply exhausted all of her energy. Brian as well was felt too weak to stand.

"Princess, any last words?" asked Haller, grinning demonically.

Haller raised the glass over his head, prepared to thrust it down into Cindy's chest. Brian watched this in horror.

Suddenly an ear-bursting roar emitted from the hole. A black arm, easily the size of a tree trunk, reached out, grasping; it was Un. He was tired of waiting.

Haller never had time to react. He was standing closest to the hole. The giant hand grabbed him and lifted him into the air. Brian could hear Haller's arms and ribs breaking in the demon's grip. They sounded like twigs.

Haller's eyes bulged out of their sockets. Blood poured from his mouth. The demon Un pulled Haller into the hole where Haller's final screams could be heard echoing. The hole then collapsed, sealing Haller away with his precious God-King.

Brian found himself able to stand. The few remaining cultist decided that they too had seen enough. They ran for the exit without looking back. Brian walked slowly over to Cindy. She seemed to be unconscious. He picked her up in his arms and walked out of the church.

As he left the church, he heard the voice of his brother whisper to him one last time.

"You did good Brian, very good. I love you kid."

"Joe, you saved me back there, thank you so much. I love you too, I love you forever Joseph."

Brian carried Cindy back to his car. Once he got her in the passenger seat, she began to stir, and finally opened her eyes and looked at him.

"Brian, you came back for me..." she spoke, her voice barely a whisper.

"Well, yeah. I've got a big brother that would have kicked my ass if I'd left you back there."

Cindy laughed softly and took Brian's hand in her own.

The police spent months investigating the church. Each and every room of The Foundation was torn apart by the cops and even the FBI.

None of the escaped members of the church were ever caught although there was a rash of suicides shortly after in the Greenwich area. In all the suicides, a single note was found with the body.

“We failed,” was written on each note.

While the Foundation members were telling the truth about Cindy’s mother having cancer, they were very wrong about their money being her only hope.

After months passed and things returned to normal, the Lawrence Group, a Non-profit Organization run by a certain very wealthy Greenwich family, paid for Cindy’s mother to be treated at the finest private hospitals available.

After college, when the time came, Brian and Cindy became husband and wife.

They named their first child Joseph and called him Joe Junior most of the time. When Joe Junior was old enough to start throwing the football around with his dad, Brian introduced him to what he called, "a very important family tradition."

Brian always let his son be Joe Montana.

Love Always

K. Banning Kellum

Friendship is compelling. So is hunger.

I am now sitting in our empty apartment. Well, I guess empty isn't really the right word. I mean, I am here, so is my best friend, no, empty isn't right I guess.

Sorry, words aren't my strong suit. I don't think as clearly as you do. I am trying to though... trying to figure all of this out. We've been in here, like this, for what seems like an eternity to me. Of course, time doesn't work as well for me as it does for you, so try to bear with me.

I am going to have to make a difficult decision soon. I have been fighting it for what I believe are six or seven days or so. Like I said, time is not easy for me to understand. I think my best friend is dead though. At first I thought he was just sleeping. Sometimes I would sleep in his room with him unless he had company over.

I guess a little back story is in order though. My thoughts are really jumbled most of the time. I mean, I know how to take care of myself for the most part, but I often struggle to put my thoughts in order.

My name is Chase. I came from a large family, but I always felt that my mother didn't love me. At first, she always made sure that my siblings, and I were fed and taken care of, but as time passed, I saw her less and less. Eventually she wouldn't even acknowledge me.

That was around the time I met Ryan, my best friend. He came by and right away we just hit it off. His mother and father really liked me too. They invited me to their house; we had dinner together, and Ryan and I would play for hours and hours. Sometimes we would play sports outside; sometimes we would just hang out in his room. He loved video games. I could never quite get the knack of the games, the controller just seemed like it wasn't designed for my hands, but that didn't stop me from sitting next to Ryan and cheering him on as he played. His joy was my joy after all.

Before I knew it, we were spending all of our time together. I loved Ryan. I knew he was my best friend. One day, we were walking to school, when another boy, his name I never knew, approached Ryan. This boy looked like trouble. He began to talk very closely to Ryan, right in his face. At first I just stood back, watching this unfold. Then the boy pushed Ryan down.

Something in me just snapped. I lunged at the boy. Other people came running across the street. I was pulled off and restrained. They took me away and locked me up for a day. I am not sure what happened to me during that time, I simply remember being terrified. As I said though, I have always had difficulty with time, and it seemed an eternity. Then, like magic, I was back with Ryan and his family again. My own mother, I can barely remember her now, never even came by to see what happened.

I loved Ryan, and after that incident, I also knew it was my job to protect Ryan. He was a great kid, but weak. He needed me. I knew this, so did he. We were a team. Ryan and Chase. Best friends. I loved him.

A very long time passed, and Ryan and I both grew older. Ryan changed in many ways, becoming distant for a time. We didn't hang out as much, and a lot of times, when I would invite him to play, he would push me away.

Eventually Ryan got old enough to move out of his parent's house, and can you believe that he invited me to move into his new apartment with him? I was so overjoyed. I still loved him. I still wanted only to protect him. Now we could live together forever. I could never ask for anything more.

Then it happened. What may have been six days ago, could be longer though. Ryan came home late. He had been with the bad people. I could smell them on his clothes. He had also been drinking that bad tasting stuff again. He had made me drink some of it with him once. It tasted awful and made it hard for me to walk. I wanted to be angry at him for making me drink it with him, but I loved him after all. With love, forgiveness is just a natural thing.

This time though, Ryan was acting like he drank a lot of it. He was stumbling around. I ran over to him; I wanted to help him to his bed, but he pushed me away. He stumbled a bit further, and then he fell. His head struck the corner of the coffee table. I could see his blood. The smell was awful.

I ran over to him and tried to wake him back up. I cried. He didn't move. I stood over him all night.

The next day, he was still sleeping on the floor. At least the terrible odor was fading. I tried to wake him up again, but he wouldn't move. He felt cold. I ate a bit of lunch and came back. He was still sleeping. It got dark again. I slept on the floor next to him, wanting to be right there when he finally woke up.

There is no food left in our apartment; at least, none that I can prepare. However, when I woke up today, next to Ryan's still body, I thought I smelled something delicious for just a moment. It passed though.

I am not sure how long it's been now. Like I keep saying, time has always confused me. I know the source of that delicious smell though. It's Ryan. He smells amazing. All of his scents are pouring out. For just a moment today, I looked at his body, which I now understand is dead, and all I saw was food. Delicious food. I am so hungry too. Now I must make my choice. I have given up on any help coming. I guess no one loved Ryan as much as I do. No one has come to see where he has been.

I wish I could cry. My eyes don't tear up though. I feel a sadness that is beyond description. Words were always hard for me; I just lived life as my gut told me. Ryan smells so delicious. I am so hungry. I suppose, in this way at least, we can always be together.

I give his face a few final licks. I whimper and whine a little, hoping that perhaps he just might wake up. I know that won't happen though. He isn't Ryan anymore, now he is just food.

I use my nose to nudge his shirt up from his soft stomach. That is where I will start. My collar jingles as I sit down on my haunches and prepare to take the first bite. I tell Ryan goodbye in the same way I always did when he would leave to go to school; him walking out to the bus; me sitting on the front porch, wagging my tail. I utter a soft bark.

I will always love you Ryan. I hope that when this is over, you'll still think of me as a good dog.

Of Beauties and Beasts

K. Banning Kellum

Beauty is shallow. So is sanity.

Kenneth Mathers loved Beauty; he adored the very aspect that Beauty presented, for all loved Beauty. Beauty was welcomed in every gathering, celebrated by the people and requested in all circles. Beauty was perfection, something that Kenneth valued and swore to protect with his life. Beauty was Kenneth's duty, a duty that he intended to carry out.

However, the Beast had other ideas. The Beast has been stalking Beauty for years, right out in plain sight. Kenneth tried to tell others about it, tried to point out the Beast.

We're getting ahead of ourselves though, aren't we?

Kenneth now in his mid-thirties and fully aware of the Beast and his evil, wicked attacks. Perhaps it first showed itself to Kenneth when he was in the 2nd or 3rd grade. Oddly enough, Beauty entered his life around the same time. Both were very close acquaintances. It was Kenneth's classmates that first made him aware of the Beast, for they saw him too. They pointed him out to Kenneth one day, explaining in small detail what he looked like and what his impact on his victim's lives caused. They whispered about the him around Kenneth from time to time. It was an ugly fiend to be sure, something to avoid. That same year, Kenneth met Beauty, and quickly became aware that they would always be hunted and terrorized by the Beast.

As years went by, Kenneth was forced to stand witness as the attacks continued. Sometimes they were minor, just some annoyance or another, intended to detract away from Beauty's ability to live and be happy. Other times, the attacks came direct and vicious, causing weeks of damage.

Kenneth tried many times to point out the Beast. He tried to tell his mother about it, to express the sheer terror that the Beast imposed. His mother would reply the same each time, telling Kenneth that he imagined all of these things, that there was no Beast.

He had photographs of it though, plenty of them. It was pale; had crooked teeth and matted hair. It looked so weak, so pitiful, yet it could cause nothing but pain and torture. Kenneth truly hated that damned evil bastard, yet despite his best efforts he could not defeat him. He tried to show his photos to others, but they pretended as though they did not see. They would chuckle and tell Kenneth that he was being ridiculous.

Life continued and Kenneth's hatred of the Beast evolved into something deeper and darker with each passing year. Beauty was becoming weaker, more distressed, begging Kenneth for help. Yet no help seemed to come.

Kenneth married the love of his life, hoping that she would dispel the influence of the Beast. For a while that worked well, and its constant harassment of Beauty slowed for a time.

However as Kenneth was driving to work one day, he looked into his rear view mirror and caught sight of the Beast. It was just there for a second, but he knew it when he saw it. It was out there, stalking yet again.

A year later the Beast was back to his old tricks. Kenneth tried so hard to get his wife to see it. He pointed it out, screamed at her to admit she could see it, and begged her to acknowledge what he saw almost every single day. She became distressed because she felt that his obsession was becoming dangerous. She tried to reassure him time and time again that there was no such thing, yet Kenneth could not look away from it. As time marched on, it seemed to grow in power, attacking directly and without mercy.

Eventually his wife left. She simply could not tolerate his fascination with the Beast any longer.

He had a photograph of it that he took recently. He sat alone in his home studying it, falling deeper and deeper into his intense hatred of the monster. It was that day that he decided to confront the Beast once and for all, ending its evil games and to rescue Beauty for good.

He was in his own home, turning towards his bedroom when he caught sight of it. The bastard was right there, invading his most private of sanctuary. It was staring at him, daring him to make a move against it. However, the Beast had made one fatal mistake; it allowed itself to be cornered. Kenneth reached for the nearest weapon he could grab, a hammer, and advanced on the intruder without fear.

“I fucking hate you!” Kenneth screamed as he walked up to it. It refused to back down; it stood its ground, inviting Kenneth to do his worst. It was mocking him as always.

“I hate everything about you; I hate your fucking crooked teeth! Why can’t they be straight, why can’t they look like everyone else’s? Normal people have straight fucking teeth!”

Kenneth attacked the Beast with the hammer, smashing its teeth, watching its mouth bleed. It felt amazing. For so many years Kenneth had wanted to go after this thing, this creature that lived only to destroy the innocent Beauty. In his glorious rage he simply couldn't understand why he'd waited so long.

Best of all, he could tell that it was feeling pain, all the pain it had inflicted coming back to it with interest.

"I hate your fucking hair! Your hair is never right. Other people, normal people, comb their hair the way they want. You piece of shit, you have to be difficult all the fucking time don't you?"

Kenneth dropped the hammer and grabbed the wounded Beast's hair and began to rip it out in great handfuls. The pain registering on its face was a vision of triumph. All the years that Kenneth had to endure this fucker's abuse of Beauty, and now it was its turn to feel that agony. Kenneth ripped its hair out until there was nothing left but a few strands and a bloody scalp. Kenneth was a warrior, Kenneth was invincible, and the Beast was finally being brought to justice.

"Let's see that scrawny little body of yours shall we? Why can't you be like everyone else, why can't you just be like everyone fucking else? Do you like being an ugly piece of shit? Is that it? Do you enjoy what you do to Beauty? Do you like the pain you inflict? Is this fun for you?"

Kenneth looked around and found a pair of sharp scissors on his bathroom sink. Sheers, used for cutting hair. Sharp as razors. Of course, since Kenneth relieved the Beast of his disgraceful excuse for a head of hair, he found another purpose for them. He began to cut the Beast's arms, slicing into the small biceps that never developed muscle or toned. The agony on its face was heavenly to Kenneth's eyes.

This moment, the moment of finally moving against the Beast, finally applying the payback that it deserved sent Kenneth into a spinning cyclone of bliss. He was alive for the first time since the bastard first introduced itself into his life.

Kenneth had to share this with his wife. She was only a few blocks away at her mother's house. One phone call and she'd be over in a matter of minutes. Finally, he could prove to her that he wasn't crazy. He had the Beast, right in front of him, wounded and bleeding. She would finally see it and she would take him back, and Beauty, his sworn charge, would finally be safe.

"Hello?" his wife answered.

"I've finally captured the Beast! I am going to kill the fucker right here. Come home and see it, come home and witness the victory of Beauty!"

"Ken, are you okay? What did you do?"

"Come home baby, come home and see for yourself, please, I love you. There is a lot of blood though, this thing bleeds after all, so, don't freak out okay?"

He was going to say more, but he looked towards his prey and saw that it was on its feet and smiling. The fucker had the nerve to still grin; just like in all those photos that Kenneth had taken. It was still making a mockery of him. Beauty was still in danger. Kenneth hung up the phone. He knew this was going to take more drastic measures. He ran into his bedroom and quickly rummaged through his closet. That's when he found what he wanted. His Colt Python revolver - fully loaded with Beast slaying glory.

"Hey fucker; still smiling?" Kenneth screamed as he turned around.

The monster had followed him. It was in his bedroom, standing against the wall, smiling and daring him to make another move. It was so hideous, so evil.

"You've hunted for your last day Beast, no more. 33 fucking years of you, every day!"

The Beast did not respond.

“You don’t know what you've put Beauty through, what you've put me through, do you? Every fucking day, you're always there, reminding us just how weak we are, reminding us that we can never be like everybody fucking else. You don’t give a damn? Well enough is enough, you don’t control me anymore!”

Kenneth aimed the gun at the fiend's head and fired one shot. He was too close to miss, and the Beast was no more.

Sharon Mathers arrived to the house with two police officers 20 minutes later. She had become concerned that her husband was unstable based on the comments he had made on that last phone call. She didn’t know what he intended to do, but she didn’t want to confront him alone.

The police entered first with their pistols drawn. They were in the house for about 15 minutes when they came out and beckoned Sharon to enter. They looked pale. Kenneth Mathers was lying on his bedroom floor in front of a full-length mirror, apparently the victim of suicide by a self-inflicted gunshot wound. He had mutilated his body quite badly before shooting himself.

Hoy Rod

K. Banning Kellum

Inspired by the song Goi, Rode, Goi from the band Arokona.

NOLA.COM: STRANGE AND EERIE FORUMS

February 5th, 2018

MuldervsScully: Hey guys, Mulder here. Anyone have a clue what these 'hoy rod' tags mean that keep showing up in New Orleans East? Just wondering.

HumanPower: Sorry dude, no clue.

PedicabPete: Haven't noticed, but I don't really spend any time in the east. Could be a gang maybe?

MuldervsScully: I thought that too, but the tag is all the way out on that weird overpass on the 1-10. You know, the one that doesn't go anywhere. It's painted on there about two dozen times.

Demonatrix: I have to go out to Slidell tomorrow, I'll look for it when I go past the overpass. Which one is it; there are two of them.

MuldervsScully: The second one if you're coming into the city, first one if you're going out I guess.

EMAIL FROM DEMONATRIX TO MULDERVSSCULLY

February 6th, 2018

Dear Mulder,

I went out to Slidell to visit my grandparents today. Real exciting stuff; right? They made me take them over to the Slidell Factory Outlet Mall. That place is still in business somehow. They have a Hudson's Treasure Hunt there though.

Anyway, I looked for your graffiti as promised. 'Hoy Rod' was all over that bridge. My brother works for the Orleans Parish Sheriff's Office. I called him and asked if there were any known gangs in their database that used such a tag. He told me he'd never heard of it.

It's probably just some bored kids or something.

Take it sleazy,

Gina

EMAIL FROM MULDERVSSCULLY TO DEMONATRIX

February 6th, 2018

Dear Gina,

Thanks for checking it out for me. I want to go out and get some pictures of it before the city paints over it. I think it'll go good in my book. Remember, you promised to buy the first copy.

Always sleazy (for you)

Mulder

FROM LANGNIAPPE MAGAZINE

Outlaw Photography a Booming Business

Today we are proud to sponsor local New Orleans 'outlaw' photographer and all around super talent behind a lens, a man who actually needs quite a bit of introduction but will probably never grant it, the mystery on your coffee table who will boggle your mind and win your heart. No one knows the real identity of this New Orleans native who first came to fame with his (or her) high risk photos taken from the top of the long neglected and very much out of service rollercoaster at the abandoned Six Flags theme park in New Orleans East. These days there are pictures all over the Internet taken from cell phones and cameras from the top of the Mega Zephyr, but as with any great art form, someone had to do it first. That person was kind enough to allow us to conduct an interview, through email of course, sticking with the pseudonym that we all know and love.

LANGIAPPE: So, why MuldervsScully? Are you an X-Files fan?

MVS: Somewhat. It started as just an email address and occasional AOL screen name, but when I started posting some of my earlier photos, I used that name. Maybe I should have picked a better Internet handle, who knows? It's what everyone knows me as now, so I guess we're stuck.

LANGIAPPE: You became famous for trespassing and taking pictures, is that a fair assessment?

MVS: As fair as it's going to get I suppose.

LANGIAPPE: Your picture from atop the Zephyr essentially brought you into the spotlight; can you tell us about some of your other works?

MVS: Of course! I recently found a way into the underground tunnels that run underneath downtown New Orleans. Those were some amazing pictures down there, like our own little catacombs. I also discovered the 'secret bridge' in City Park, the one that goes over to Goldfish Island. What I am most proud of though is getting into the ruins of Sheriff Foti's Haunted House attraction. Hard to believe that they just left it all standing. Look for some really cool shots of left over props and such.

LANGIAPPE: We understand that you have a new coffee table book coming out this year. Can you clue us in one what your next big angle is going to be?

MVS: The base theme is going to be 'mysteries.' All those weird little things in our city that we've all seen since we were kids but never really knew the stories behind will be the chief concept. Everything from that strange little castle house in Irish Bayou, the two overpasses on the 1-10 that don't lead to anything, the gutter punk subculture in the French Quarter and anything else that we've always wanted to know more about. I'm going to explain as much as I can through photos.

Right now I'm especially interested in exploring the roots of some graffiti that pops up in the more rural sections of the city.

LANGIAPPE: Any chances of a face reveal this time?

MVS: Maybe if I get to 5 million followers on Instagram... maybe.

EMAIL FROM MULDERVSSCULLY TO DEMONTATRIX

February 9th, 2018

Hey Gina,

I'm heading out there today to get some pictures and explore around a bit. Wish me luck!

Mulder

NOLA.COM: STRANGE AND EERIE FORUMS

Muldervsscully: Hey guys! So I drove out to that overpass in the East today. I parked my car on the shoulder and got some great pictures of the "Hoy Rod" tags all over the bridge. It was so bizarre! The tag was covering almost every piece of concrete and steel available. I even found it underneath the overpass on the underside of the bridge. From where it was painted it would almost seem like someone would have had to set up a ladder to reach it.

Anyway, it gets better. I decided to take a hike down the exit ramp. Believe it or not I've never actually explored back there despite the million or so times I must have driven past it.

The street was in bad shape. I doubt it could have been driven on without some serious off-roading capabilities. Sadly, my little Volvo isn't built for such. Even though the sun was out and everything was bright and cheery, I had the worst sensations of... well, 'being watched.' I know that sounds cliché and all, but honestly it's what I felt back there. I probably just let the whole strange tag thing get into my head a little, but seriously, I honestly felt creeped out the entire time I was back there. Keep in mind this is coming from a guy who specializes in getting pictures in places where I'm not supposed to be.

I did get some good pictures while I was back there though to go along with the 'Hoy Rod' bridge images. I'll share a few on here later!

EMAIL FROM DEMONATRIX TO MULDERVSSCULLY

February 10th 2018

Yo Mulder!

I read your post on NOLA! I'd love to see some of those pictures that you got! If you weren't into this anonymous shtick, I'd totally go out there with you to protect you from the big bad ghosties that were bothering you lol. Keep me in the loop bro!

Sleazily yours,

Gina

EMAIL FROM MULDERVSSCULLY TO DEMONATRIX

February 10th 2018

Gina my muse! Maybe one day you'll be the face whom which I reveal my face. Anyway, I've decided to go back out there at night. I want to get some shots of the area that set a better 'mood' and honestly the bright and sunny day setting doesn't exactly convey what I want. I've attached a couple of the pictures from my first trip out there though. More to come!

Yours in sleaze,

Mulder

EMAIL FROM DEMONATRIX TO MULDERVSSCULLY

February 10th 2018

Hey Mulder,

No joke here. Did you notice that 'person' in black in the woods in the third pic you sent me? It was taken I guess from the exit ramp once you were out there in the woods. I noticed it almost right away so I know you must have seen it. It looks… almost like a Halloween witch? That's the best way I can describe it. The body shape looks vaguely feminine (just going off of the waist and hips) and it's wearing all black. I've gone ahead and zoomed in and cropped just that portion. I'm sure you have better editing software than I do, but it's worth checking out. Unless this is all part of your 'art' in which case, fuck you! J/K. But still, really creepy. If this wasn't one purpose, I'd suggest checking it out, someone might be stalking you!

No sleaze—too creeped out,

Gina

NOLA.COM: STRANGE AND EEIRE FORUMS

February 11th 2018

Muldervsscully: There is nothing out there.

HumanPower: What do you mean? Like, nothing worth photographing?

TomThumb009: I think he logged out.

BBumbler18: Mulder…? Hello???

HumanPower: Just an artist acting artsy. He's probably just building suspense.

PedicabPete: Still, it's not like him to just pop in and pop out. Vague isn't his style.

Demonatrix: I'll email him. There was something odd in some pictures that he sent me. I reached out to him earlier, but he hasn't written me back yet. Also out of character for him.

TomThumb009: So it is a 'he!' One mystery solved!

Demonatrix: Actually I don't know. As long as we've been chatting privately Mulder has never given me much info about his… OR HER, personal life.

BBumbler18: Well shit girl, you're supposed to be our MOLE! LOL!!

Demonatrix: Oh wait, I just got an email from Mulder! Let me do my 'mole' duties!

EMAIL FROM MULDERVSSCULLY TO DEMONATRIX

February 11th, 1971

There is nothing out there. There is nothing anywhere. There is nothing, nothing, nothing, nothing, nothing, nothing, nothing, nothing, nothing, nothing, nothing… Hoy Rod.

EMAIL FROM DEMONATRIX TO MULDERVSSCULLY

February 11th, 2018

Okay, I'm guessing this is part of the act? I see you attached the night pictures to that last "message" you sent me. I like the creep-factor but come on Mulder; you don't have to treat me like one of your fans.

I would like to know how you altered the dates on the email time-stamp though. That's some next level shit! Very eerie; for real though, please just let me know you're okay. I'm not trying to get all mushy here, but your last few posts on NOLA and that email you sent me (weird date and all) just don't seem like the usual 'you.' Do me this favor and I promise I'll go back to regarding you with the typical apathetic nature of a fellow citizen of the Internet.

Gina

NOLA.COM: STRANGE AND EERIE FORUMS

February 12th, 2018

Demonatrix: Has anyone else heard from Mulder lately? He sent me an email right after his weird little post last night. It was strange. He sent more pictures and they are really freaking me out. I'm not sure if this is some elaborate marketing thing he's doing or not though, so I'm not going to share any of the pictures on here without his permission, but still… I'm a bit worried, anyone know anything?

HumanPower: Not a thing Demon.

PedicabPete: You're asking us? You're his favorite… lol! But for real, if you hear from him, let us know.

BBumbler08: What was so strange about the latest pictures? Can you give us some information at least?

Demonatrix: I'll say this much, the pics that he sent me were of places that shouldn't even be there. I don't know, maybe he found something out there that I never knew about, but still, it's all very strange.

My uncle and his pals used to hunt out there a lot and they told me they've never seen anything out there like what Mulder photographed. Hopefully he comes out of hiding and clears this up.

HumanPower: Okay, now you're just being EVIL! What did he send you?

Demonatrix: Give it a few more days. I don't want to ruin his project if it turns out that this is what it is. He trusts me and I'd hate to betray that. I have my fingers crossed that he pops back up and announces that this was all some weird little campaign to get attention for his next book. I won't keep you guys in the dark much longer though, I promise.

EMAIL FROM DEMONATRIX TO PROFESSOR ROSE LOGGINS.LSU

February 14th, 2018

Dear Professor Loggins,

I hope you remember me (and don't hold the silly email handle against me) but this is Gina DeLuna from your Louisiana History class from 2012. I can't go into too much detail here, but I'm sort of friends with a local photographer who is well known as MuldervsScully. Not sure if you're familiar with him/her or not, but he specializes in what is called 'outlaw' photography. Anyway, we've been corresponding for a long time now and recently he went out to photograph some graffiti on one of the abandoned overpasses in New Orleans East. Something about the tag really fascinated him I think.

Either way, right after his first trip out there he started acting strange. The pictures he's sent me are really unusual as well. Some locations just don't seem as though they should be there off of the Interstate. I don't want to post any of them publically since this could still be part of his exhibit, but I'd really appreciate it if you could look at them and tell me anything at all that I might not know.

Thanks a million!

Geaux Tigers,

Gina DeLuna

LSU Alumni Class of 2014

EMAIL FROM ROSE LOGGINS.LSU TO DEMONATRIX

February 15th, 2018

Dear Gina,

It's always great to hear from one of my past students. I hope you're putting that degree of yours to work! Anyway, I looked at the picture you sent me and yes, I do have some information for you. I'll go line by line here, and of course add some history of the 'abandoned overpasses' as well. Since you expressed that you wish to keep this off the radar, I'll respect that and will not share anything contained in our communications. Just be aware that if your friend is in some sort of trouble, it is your ethical duty to report it to the authorities. You may lose a friend but you might also save a life. Enough soap boxing though, let's dig into these photos:

First of all, your friend is some sort of genius if this is all a work. The time-stamps on all the pictures (contained within the details) are set to 1971. That is the year that those overpasses were built; with the idea being at the time that the oil market in New Orleans East would last forever. Sadly we all know that didn't happen. The goal of the project was to develop massive subdivisions back there. The entire area was going to be known as "Orlandia." However, when the oil industry dried up the city no longer had the money to keep going, so the overpasses became nothing more than giant loops that led to nothing.

Now that history class is over, let's talk geography. The locations in the pictures did exist; at least, they did back in the 70's.

I'll label the pictures as he did for ease of access:

1. World of Dead Rocks

The first picture that he sent you show a small grove off of the exit ramp. In it can be seen a formation of strange, tall rocks. Some of them appear to go up at least 20 feet high.The history of the rocks is not 100% clear, as they do not form naturally in Louisiana nor are they a part of any landscape in this state. They were discovered in the 70's when the first crews went out there to survey the land. For a short time they were known as the "Cajun Stonehenge" and a few people offered to buy them when the city decided it was best to just clear them out to make way for the exit ramp. Where they came from or who put them out, there will likely forever be a mystery although I can still remember my older brother telling me ghost stories about the rocks. He said that they were built by a coven of devil worshipers to summon demons. That's a sibling for you though.

2. Crazy Waters

The second picture shows a small bayou that extends almost to the road. I believe what you're looking at here is a portion of Bayou Sauvage. To make way for the ramp, this area was drained. A bit of creepy history though, several bodies were found down there when that particular section was cleaned out. I think the city kept the discoveries as quiet as possible so as not to disrupt the very expensive project that they were undertaking. This body of water, like the rocks, has been gone since the 70's.

3. House of Rod

This one is actually a bit of a mystery to me. Your friend appears to have captured the image of a small church out there. There were people living out there at the time, but most of them lived in the little 'swamp shacks' lined up along the bayou. They'd use small rowboats and the like to get to the road when they needed to come into the city.While it is possible that this community constructed a small church for Sunday worship so they could avoid having to trek into the city, I certainly cannot find any records. The building in the picture would far more likely have been a hunter's shack used for hanging carcasses, however, the design of the structure along with what I can see are stained glass windows doesn't really support my theory, now does it?

As far as the reference to "House of Rod" I once again have nothing to go on. With your permission I'd like to forward the image of the church to one of my colleagues in our Theology department. Perhaps this 'Rod' is some long lost religious sect out there.

Well Gina, that is the best I can do at the moment. I hope you're able to get in contact with your friend soon. As far as the pictures themselves, they must be the product of some very talented photo alterations. My guess is that this photographer got ahold of some very rare, very old images from before the overpasses were built and applied a bit of computer voodoo to make them appear to exist in the present along the exit ramp. I can assure you though that never in life did the exit ramp and any of those structures exist at the same time.

Best of luck,

Professor Loggins

EMAIL FROM MULDERVSSCULLY TO DEMONATRIX

February 16th, 1971

Hoy Rod, Hoy Rod, Hoy Rod, Hoy Rod.

IMAGE ATTACHED

EMAIL FROM DEMONATRIX TO MULDERVSSCULLY

February 16th, 2018

Mulder,

I'm not sure if this is all part of your project or not, but enough is enough. I thought that we were friends… or at least something more than just a fan and an artist. Either way, the last picture that you sent me was very inappropriate and disturbing. Perhaps I thought that I was deeper into this form or art than I really am or maybe I was just taken by the fact that a photographer that I really respected was taking the time to talk to me as a person.

Either way, I want off of this ride. I'm worried about you because you won't give me any straight answers and you keep sending me these weird photos. The last one though… it's just more than I signed on for. I'd love to still support your work and correspond with you but if this is just a stunt to promote your work or something, I have to tell you I find it pretty shitty that you'd treat me like some blind audience member.

Unless you're willing to drop this act and tell me what is really going on, then I must ask that you stop emailing me.

Gina

NOLA.COM: STRANGE AND EERIE FORUMS

February 17th, 2018

Muldervsscully: IMAGES UPLOADED

HumanPower: Dude! Amazing stuff! Are you sure you want to post this on here though? Someone might steal it!

PedicabPete: If this is what he's giving away for free then I bet the actual book is going to be AMAZING!

BBumbler08: That is very disturbing stuff Mulder! You are a genius!

Rod: HE SLEEPS NO MORE!

HumanPower: Hello Rod, new to the forums? Are you a fan of Mulder?

BBumbler08: Creepy!

PedicabPete: All part of the act I bet!

Muldervsscully: They have no eyes here... yet they see it all.... HOY ROD!!

NOLASTAFF: The images recently posted by user Muldervsscully violate our Content Policy regarding depictions of extreme violence. The pictures will be removed and you will receive a warning. Please review our Content Policy before posting images in the future.

EMAIL FROM JOHN.LANDIS.LSU TO DEMONATRIX

February 17th, 2018

Dear Gina,

I hope you forgive Professor Loggins and myself here, but she went ahead and showed me some images that you sent to her regarding your friend's adventures in photography. I happen to have a bit of information on the topic though, especially in regard to the reference to 'Rod.' I certainly hope this doesn't overstep any trust and I assure you that I will not share any of this information publically although I must say it would make one fascinating article. (Or perhaps horror movie!)

The Cult of Rod existed in the bayou area outside of New Orleans for quite a while before the Interstate was put in. Keep in mind that during much of the early 20th century, the only way to access the North Shore (Slidell side) from New Orleans was by way of the Highway 11 Bridge over Lake Pontchartrain. However, during 60's when the East became a big oil beacon the 1-10 was constructed to include the Twin Span that connects New Orleans and the Irish Bayou area to Slidell.

Not too much is known about the Rod Cult other than the fact that they were very territorial and very secretive. Hunters knew to avoid their stomping grounds and occasionally a strange altar or other weird artifacts would be discovered. People didn't disturb their religious icons though. When the two 'abandoned overpasses' were constructed though, road crews were given strict instructions to dismantle any obstructions. The 'dead stones' and 'church of rod' that your friend photographed were indeed discovered and removed during this time.

For this act of sacrilege there were repercussions, at least according to local lore. During the construction project, vehicles were said to catch on fire for no apparent reason. There was one story that claimed a man's chainsaw burst into flames as he was cutting down a tree. The 'dead stones' themselves claimed at least four lives as one crushed a worker as they were attempting to move them. A vehicle hauling the stones allegedly fell off of the High Rise Bridge in Gentilly, killing the driver. Even after the project was completed the foreman of the road crew suffered a major heart attack.

An 'urban legend' or sorts circulated for a short time that the Cult of Rod cursed the entire city. Curses or not, the group vanished shortly after the construction of the overpasses was complete. Until now anyway, no one has mentioned that odd little footnote from New Orleans' esoteric past.

In all truth I wouldn't worry too much about this. I looked into your friend's portfolio and all of this behavior seems to follow what appears to be his standard of strange and provocative imagery. My guess would be that this is one big marketing blitz on his part to pull his potential audience into the book. He very well may have painted those 'hoy rod' markings on the overpass himself just to create the buzz.

If I can be of any further assistance, please feel free to reach out. Best of luck!

Sincerely,

Professor John Landis

Department of Theology

Louisiana State University

EMAIL FROM MULDERVSSCULLY TO DEMONATRIX

<Google Unable to time-stamp>

Help me. Rod is awake.

VIDEO ATTACHED

EMAIL FROM DEMONATRIX TO MULDERVSSCULLY

February 18th, 2018

I'm going to the police. You can hate me if you want to Mulder, but this is scaring me.

Gina

FROM TIMES PICAYUNE EARLY EDITION:

LOCAL PHOTOGRAPHER MISSING AFTER SHARING TERRIFYING VIDEO WITH FRIEND

February 19th, 2018

In a story that is still being investigated by the New Orleans Police Department, local 'outlaw' photographer William Darsow, known around the Internet and book stores as Muldervsscully is missing and presumed in great danger. Darsow, whose identity has been a long held secret, was uncovered during the viewing of a video that he shared with a friend. His email records also reveal his true identity.

The authorities became aware of this situation after a friend of Darsow's, Gina DeLuna of New Orleans alerted the police that she believed her friend was in danger. According to DeLuna, Darsow had been investigating graffiti on the overpass located on the I-10 between New Orleans East and Slidell. She stated that the project began as most of Darsow's had in the past but quickly took a turn for the unsettling when he stopped communicating with her as they normally did but rather begin to share disturbing photographs believed to be taken in the area of the overpass.

According to DeLuna, two images drove her to report the activity to police. The first alarming photograph shows what appear to be several women dressed in what could be called traditional Halloween 'witch' costumes conducting some sort of ritual around a stone altar. The women are wearing all black and even sport the long pointed hats often associated with the witch theme.

The second image shows several of these 'witches' surrounding the photographer. From the perspective of the photograph, it appears that Darsow was on the ground looking up. The image is particularly unnerving as it appears that these women do not have faces and that the pointed hats actually seem to form from their heads as opposed to be worn.

DeLuna confirmed that she was hesitant to report this matter at first as she believed this could all be a marketing attempt as Darsow was intending to publish a new book of photography in the near future. However, a video that he sent to her email account less than 24 hours ago finally convinced her to step forward.

The video, which has been deemed too disturbing and graphic to be posted on our streaming webpage, came with the caption 'help me.' According to those that have viewed the video though (both DeLuna and the officers investigating the matter) it appears to show Darsow being held down on the same stone altar from previous photos while he is being mutilated. The phrase 'Hoy Rod' can be heard in the background of the video apparently being chanted by those in attendance.

DeLuna and others have stated that they are still holding out hope that this is one very elaborate commercial for Darsow's book and that he will emerge unharmed. We will continue to cover this story and report any new developments.

FROM LANGIAPPE MAGAZINE

June 2nd, 2018

In a few days the final published works of New Orleans photographer William Darsow will be released to book stories nationwide. For those of you not following local news this year, Darsow was found dead near the 1-10 overpasses in New Orleans East several months ago. The identities of those responsible for this death remain a mystery and no further leads have developed since the horrific and heartbreaking murder of this young and talented artist.

In March of this year a package arrived at the publishing house, which Darsow was contracted. It contained a stack of photographs (some from his final investigation into the 'hoy rod' graffiti) and instructions to posthumously publish what would be his final book. A national release is scheduled for June 7th.

FROM MULTIPLE NEWS SOURCES

June 7th, 2018

New Orleans: 11 people are dead today after a strange and unexplainable illness at a Metairie bookstore saw people begin to convulse and...

Tampa, Florida: At a highly anticipated book release today a mysterious illness claimed the lives of at least 18 attendees...

Austin, Texas: A downtown bookstore burst into flames today during a highly anticipated...

Atlanta, Georgia: No survivors as bookstore roof collapses during release of...

Santa Monica, California: 16 dead as massive sinkhole appears at bookstore...

Providence, Rhode Island: Flames continue to pour from the windows of a small bookseller despite the efforts of fire fighters. At least a dozen people are believed to be inside…

Dinner with Vivianna

K. Banning Kellum

We're halfway there folks, let's laugh a little!

As far back as I can remember, I always wanted to be a gangster… oh wait, I'm thinking of Goodfellas, let's try this again. As far back as I can remember, I always wanted a good-looking girlfriend and to be a least kind of popular. Yeah, that sounds more like it. How's everyone doing? My name is Cameron Dunn, and this is my story. Who am I speaking to? Who even knows? My pursuit for love currently has me locked up in a cage. Yep, Cameron is caged, or so it seems. Who threw me in here, and why am I currently pacing the walls… heck, how am I even writing this? Well, some answers will be revealed, I promise.

A bit about me, I was lonely. Hell, I was so lonely that the closest thing I ever had to a girlfriend came from my affinity to Julia Walker; she's the zombie girl from Return of the Living Dead 3, in case you didn't know. She's played by Melinda Clarke, and let me tell you, she made me fall in love in an hour and a half. That should sum me up a bit. I was the guy that fell in love with movie characters and would later doze off as I fantasized about fictional lives together with people that didn't even exist. Oh Julie, I would have loved you, zombie or not. My best friend is a guy named Ike Ruddock. He's a lot like me, in the lonely department. We'd sit up for hours on the phone chatting about the lives we wished we had. We're both 16 you see; guess I should have mentioned that earlier. Our long nightly ramblings would generally consist of such gems as, 'I wish we had girlfriends,' or, 'this is how life would be if we had girlfriends.' Okay, not trying to sound too much like a copy of Kenny Leonard here. Trust me, we had our own issues, and not all of them based around our crippling lack of physical contact from the opposite sex.

Neither Ike nor I were really miserable folks all the time either. We had our hobbies. Now, those hobbies consisted mainly of playing Final Fantasy 3 all night and talking about it. We also liked renting cheap horror movies and making fun of them, and of course there were our semi-regular nights of egging cars and pouring sticky drinks over payphones. Ike had his driver's license, so we'd slip out sometimes and go around doing dumb stuff like that. A good day out was a trip to the mall, waste a dozen quarters or so at the arcade and get kicked out of Toys R Us for making the talking Stone Cold Steve Austin doll say vulgar things. (Shake them titties just sounds so strange coming from a plastic Steve Austin head.) However, there was a hole there in our lives, and that hole was a girlfriend.

I think we got shot down a lot because we went after the wrong types though. For our first couple years of high school, we went after the cookie cutter "hot girl" type. This was usually the preppy, popular chick that would look at us and laugh. It wasn't until we watched a little flick called The Craft that I finally realized that the problem was we were chasing after the wrong types. Remember how I mentioned falling in love with the zombie girl from Return of the Living Dead 3? Well, let's just say that when I saw Fairuza Balk's character in The Craft, my heart spun on its head. I knew that was the key. I needed to just find some socially awkward girl who could understand and appreciate the finer nuances that I brought to the relationship table. If that girl could be as attractive as Balk's character that would just be a double win for me. Who knows, maybe even Ike could find one too and we could go on weird double dates down to the local cemetery. We could try to summon demons and then do weird stuff on graves. See folks, I was thinking clearly, and the motivation to find my odd girlfriend grew from there.

So, forgive me here, I'm working with a 5000 word limit, which sounds like a lot, but in actuality isn't, so, I'll have to forgo the massive purple prose you're obviously looking forward to, sorry. Here's the deal, Ike, and I lived in New Orleans, (of course we did, I believe it's a rule or something, we have to) and our high school, Warren Easton, was full of potential love interests. However, my idea of just finding a weird girl that would look past our obvious social shortcomings was quickly failing. Turns out that even the artsy, gothy types still had friends and interests that kept a gap between our virginity and romantic bliss. I wasn't into their music or fashion, (I actually thought Marilyn Manson was called Merlyn Manson for about 6 months and made that mistake a couple of times when trying to bond over music) and my clothes ranged from K-Mart to the bargain bin when J. C. Penney had a sale. Ike wasn't quite as on board with the 'get a strange girl' plan, as I think he was still holding out hope that Clarissa from Clarissa Explains It All was a real person that would surely crawl out of his television any day. So it was just I, failing in glorious fashion.

That is, until she transferred to our school.

Vivianna Alexander was her name. She showed up one day in class out of nowhere. She was perfect! Lovely pale skin, deep dark hair, secretive eyes, she was the Fairuza Balk to my... Well, there wasn't a male lead in that movie, so she was the Balk to my... me. She was new to the school, so she had no friends for me to compete with. Does all of this make me sound creepy? C'mon, I'm 16, how developed do you expect me to be? I saw this as a sign. So, in true Cameron fashion, I avoided her and instead tried to dig up some information. There wasn't much to dig though. Ike knew less about her than I did. All I was able to get from asking around to the few people that would speak to me was that she'd come here from another town due to family issues. I had no idea what those issues were. That would involve speaking to her, but I figured that it'd bode well for me to get to know her. After all, I had a few issues at home too. My mother was raising me alone, and she was a handful, anyway. Big old half Sicilian woman, loved to eat and talk at volumes far beyond those of normal social standards. Still though, the challenge was in talking to her, which is not something I excelled at. However, fate seemed to be on my side throughout, as a few events happened that led me right into her home.

She mutilated a bird. That's what started it. See, everyone was saying how weird she was. She would sit in silence, eat lunch alone, and walk with her head down. On paper, it would seem that her self-esteem was just low enough to make her a perfect candidate to date me. People left her alone for the most part. Some girls called her Lydia, like from Beetlejuice I guess, while a few others asked her once or twice if she worshiped Satan. That was about the extent of it though. She wasn't really focused on until the bird incident. No one knows why she did it either, and with my luck, I missed it when it happened. Kids were saying though that she was seen at lunch slicing open a bird on one of the outdoor stone tables near the cafeteria. See, Warren Easton was located about a half mile from downtown New Orleans, so we got a lot of pigeons. Most of the kids would toss them bread during lunch, so these birds knew where to come every day for a good meal. According to the rumor mill, Vivianna had managed to catch one. Kids were watching as she gently picked the bird up, laid it down on the table before her, and proceeded to use a fork (yes, a fork) to slice it open down the stomach. People watched on in shock and awe as she then dipped her finger into its open guts and took a taste of its blood.

Now, at first I thought this was all bogus. They already were calling her a devil worshipper, so the idea of her killing a bird in the name of her dark lord just seemed too convenient. I was ready to rule it out, but then Ike called me that night and told me that he saw it happen. I would have laughed at anyone else, but Ike didn't lie. He called and told me something like, "Dude, that freaky girl you like killed a bird at lunch today and drank its blood."

We talked about that for a long time, and he swore on all the characters of Final Fantasy and beyond that it happened, just like that. The next day she wasn't at school, as she'd likely been suspended, but all the kids were talking now. Those hard to find rumors were fleshing themselves out as suddenly everyone was a subject matter expert on Vivianna.

"She had to transfer from her old school because the police found out what her family really does," said one girl to me as I sat down in class.

"Her family was kidnapping local homeless people," said another.

"They were caught running a Satanic Cult and had to move out of their last neighborhood," confirmed a third.

By the end of that day I heard that she was a Satanist, a serial killer and finally even a cannibal. Someone even claimed that her father ran a restaurant that was secretly serving human to wealthy weirdos, and the cops had caught on. I didn't really believe much of it, as most of those claims should have wound her family up in jail, not just moving to another school. However, the bird incident seemed to have really happened, as not just Ike but just about everyone else that shared a lunch period with her swore they witnessed the event. There was even a little reddish-brown stain on the table where she'd been sitting. Bird blood perhaps?

Now, if you think these rumors would have deterred me away from her, you'd don't know old Cameron Dunn. She really was turning out to be like Fairuza from The Craft. We could be the weird couple of Warren Easton. The bizarre, bird-slicing Vivianna and her faithful boyfriend, the slightly chubby yet otherwise lovable Cam; it was a match made in Heaven… or somewhere at least.

She came back to school a few days later, and let me tell you all, the kids were not forgiving. I didn't know we had so many pigeon lovers there. Girls snubbed or ridiculed her, boys made the sign of the cross when she walked by, and poor little Vivianna, she walked through it all. I was actually trying to think of just the right way to approach the situation. I mean, I am pretty shy, even when it comes to talking to an animal mutilator, but around 2pm that Friday, the gods smiled upon me… sort of.

I'd come around the corner and found her surrounded by two guys and a girl. They were shouting horrible things, calling her a witch, a bitch and… well, nothing else really rhymes that works, so you get the idea. The girl was of directing the two guys. Maybe they didn't feel too good about bullying a lone girl, but their friend was providing the cheerleading, and they were following the cadence. This was my chance. Vivianna was up against the wall, trying to walk past, but the guys kept blocking her.

"You going to cast a spell on us, bitch? You going to turn us into birds?" the girl taunted. I still don't know why you'd provoke someone by daring them to cast a spell on you, but that seemed to be their game. So, feeling like Locke from Final Fantasy 3 when he bravely stepped in to protect Terra, I puffed up my chest, stepped in between them and made my stand.

I was promptly beaten up.

When I came around, I was sitting up against the wall while Vivianna was dabbing blood off of my cheek with her thumb. And you know what, I could have sworn I saw her lick her thumb at least once. I didn't care though; in my mind I'd just made the first move in Operation Fairuza.

"God, dude, why did you do that?" she'd asked.

"I didn't like seeing you getting picked on; three on one, two of them being guys, I had to say something."

"Yeah, but I'm used to it. It's like this at most schools. I stick out, it happens."

She finished her strange ritual of cleaning me up and helped me to my feet. We spent a little time that day talking after school. She told me that she was new to New Orleans; she hinted that there were some issues at her last school, but didn't go into detail. I wanted to push further, but didn't want to scare her off either. We sat out front until her parents pulled up to get her. I wanted to ask for her phone number, or at least give her mine, but it seemed as though the chance was slipping. I still could have, but that damn shyness kept holding me back. She finally gave me a hug and thanked me once more. She told me we'd talk more on Monday and briskly climbed into her parent's car.

The parents, WOW! Big black sedan, I could see her father only briefly through the open window. He was a tall looking man, black beard, black turtleneck; he looked like the father of a bird-killing cannibal. They drove off, and I sat there wishing I'd have gotten her number. However, luck was apparently on my side.

That night, it was around 8pm; I was about to call Ike up for our nightly chat about life, love and all things Square Soft, when the phone rang. My mom picked it up from the kitchen and I could hear almost every word. As I said before, she spoke as though the world was all half deaf and she was the only hope of an audible connection. She came into my room, smiling ear to ear, and informed me that I had a phone call.

It was Vivianna. We talked for a little while. Mostly mundane stuff, more thanks for stepping in at school followed by what I could only call a blessing from Heaven above, an invitation to her home the following night!

My mom filled me in on the rest. Turns out Vivianna told her parents all about my heroic intervention. Her folks were so impressed that they looked us up in the phone book and called to talk to my mother. They thanked her for the remarkable bravery of her son and extended an invitation for me to come by the following night and eat with them in their home. When I was put on the phone with Vivianna, she was really opening up. Her voice sounded almost giddy, not the drab tone maintained at school. She seemed legitimately thrilled at the idea of me coming over. I know I was!

The next night I was all set for the "date." My mom was thrilled about it too. She was always going on about how I needed to find a nice girl and be a normal teenager. Of course she insisted that I bring food. I told her that this was a dinner and food would already be there, but as I mentioned once before, my mom revolved all affection around the idea of a meal. She put something together in a Tupperware container and insisted that I offer it. I didn't think it was polite to do so, but I brought it with me at mom's insistence. She dropped me off at their home, told me to call her when it was over and left me standing there on the sidewalk in front of the Alexander home.

Okay, time to set some mood here; I know I gotta get the reader (or listener if Creeparoni gets ahold of this) into the right mindset. I was nervous now. Yes, part of it was that I was going into the home of a girl that I really liked and had to not make an ass out of myself. Another part of me though was a little nervous about all the crap I'd heard about her family. Satan worship, cannibalism and kidnappings had been the most common of rumors. Could any of that be true? These were realizations that I'd never come close to meeting up with in real life. How would I actually respond to it? Well, no sense in just standing out on the pavement wondering, it was time to go in and find out what the real deal was all about.

Her father answered the door, and just as I recalled from seeing him briefly in his car, he was an odd one. Tall as all hell, the guy had to be pushing over six feet, with a neatly cropped beard that was as black as night, and some really intense eyes.

"You must be Cameron!" he said in a voice that was a bit too jolly for his appearance. "C'mon in, we've been waiting for you!"

"Thank you for having me over," I replied with a bit of nerves.

He took the Tupperware container from me and sat it down on their dining room table. His wife came out to join him. Now, she was almost like a stereotype of the creepy parent too. This was too much. She was attractive for a woman her age. She had long blonde hair that was almost platinum, deep brown eyes and a wide smile that seemed to have too many teeth for any human jaw.

"Cameron, so nice to meet you! I'm Renee, Viv's mom, and you've already met my husband Casper!"

The dad's name was Casper… I sure hope he's friendly.

"Yes, Cameron, stay as long as you'd like… Perhaps even longer!" Casper announced, followed by a deep laugh. My skin broke out in goose bumps for just a moment.

"Casper, that joke has never been funny, stop it!" Renee scolded, and the big man blushed a bit.

I was led through to the living room, where I assumed I would get grilled a bit by the parents, and that's when I saw it all. They had two lamps, both appearing to be made of human remains. That's right, I'm skipping over the buildup and going right into their lamps. It was too much to ignore. Bones created the lamp base, and in place of a traditional shade was a thin filmy substance that I thought for sure was human flesh. It was stapled together at the seams.

"Do you like the lamps?" Renee asked me.

"Well, I..."

"I hope he likes them, they cost me a fortune," Casper replied.

"Well, dear, when you insist on buying props from popular movies, you have to spend a little."

"Props?" I was trying to hide the apprehension in my voice.

"Yep, from Texas Chainsaw Massacre! Renee and I actually saw that movie on our first date, and it's always been special to us. They filmed that movie out near Austin, TX, where we just moved from. It turns out they were selling off some old props, and when I saw those lamps, I knew I had to get them for our home."

Okay, I could breathe again.

"I feel so bad for what happened at school with Viv and that damned bird. It's all Casper's fault, you know," Renee stated.

I was about to ask for more information, what really happened, when suddenly I heard the stairs creaking from overhead, and looked up to see Vivianna herself coming down. She looked stunning. If there was ever a time in real life for that Sixpence None the Richer song "Kiss Me" to play, this was it. She was wearing a long black dress, had her hair up and was almost gliding down the stairs.

"Cameron, so glad you're here!" My heart did a little flip when our eyes locked.

Renee led us all to the table. Vivianna sat next to me. If it were possible to go to Heaven, die there, and go to like, Super Heaven, this was it.

"Let's eat!" Casper stated with excitement, maybe a bit too much, and I saw how wide and hungry his eyes became.

A domed plate was put in front of me. "Guests always go first," Renee stated and gestured for me to remove the dome.

I pulled up the dome and almost jumped from the table. On the plate in front of me was a dead bird, a pigeon.

"The culprit himself," Casper joked.

"What... what is this?"

"That's the reason our daughter is getting bullied, Casper and his antics, I swear if we have to move again..."

Vivianna reached over and grabbed it. I watched in stunned silence as she jabbed her fork down into the dead animal's stomach, producing a red liquid. Just as I'd heard she'd done at school, she dipped her finger into the pool of slime and took a lick.

"We thought it'd be funny if she brought it to school to show it off," Casper said. "Turns out not so much."

"Another of my husband's stupid props. This one we named Ozzie. It was a prop from some zombie movie. You fill the rubber bird with strawberry jelly and bite into it for effect. I guess we figured Viv could show it off, impress some friends or something. Who would've believed those kids would actually think it was real?"

"You mean, it was a fake bird?"

"Of course. What, did you think I actually killed a pigeon?"

"Well, of course I never believed it even happened, but, now that you've shown me what it really is... jeez, hard to believe people were so freaked out, right?"

Viv smiled at that. I guess I covered for myself well enough.

"My parents are both artists, Cameron, and we actually owned a studio out in Austin. Things were going well enough until my dad got the idea to do a damned over-the-top exhibit on the streets."

"Hey, that exhibit was brilliant. I created a real life horror show right there on 7th street in downtown Austin. I had a beheading, a disemboweling, all free for the public to view. It was even around Halloween. I had no idea that the police would get called out because some folks actually thought I was murdering someone on the sidewalk," Casper explained.

"So, that's why you guys had to move?" I asked.

"Yeah, the publicity didn't go over well for my dad's studio. It was meant to be a really deep art show but turned out to just freakout a lot of people. Guess the 'Keep Austin Weird' motto isn't as true as they claim."

"We always heard that New Orleans was really tolerant of the strange and eccentric, so we sold the studio and decided to try to set up shop down here. Then Casper sends our daughter to school with a prop bird filled with jelly and it looks like we're on the fast track to be pariahs again."

"Okay, enough about that, let's eat!" Vivianna suddenly exclaimed.

"I hope you like meat!" Casper announced and gave me a strange wink.

"Oh, dad, are we having dried James tonight?"

"Of course, dear!"

James?

A plate was produced with what appeared to be sliced up tubes of red meat. "Now Cameron, James here was a bit of a jerk, but he certainly will snap right into your mouth!" Renee announced.

The family tore into the tubes of meat. I sat there stunned for a moment when suddenly the tension was broken.

"I love these things!" Viv informed me. "I used to think Slim Jims were gross, but when my dad started calling them James, I don't know, it was just too funny not to enjoy."

Slim Jim's… jerky… of course. Jim is short for James; just another damned dad joke from Casper the Freaky Ghost. I ate one and was indeed informed by my mouth that this was store bought beef jerky.

"Okay, Cameron, I hope you're ready for the main course!" Casper announced. "I hope you like human!"

Okay, there it was, no way that I misheard or misunderstood that. The man just said human, as in, people.

"Yeah, we know not everyone is a big fan of human. We started eating it back in Austin though, and Viv can't get enough of it," Renee chimed in. I could see that both she and her husband had dried meat stuck to their cheeks. Their teeth now looked really sharp as they smiled.

"I'll get it!" Vivianna said with excitement. I sat there in silence.

She returned from the kitchen a moment later with a large bowl of what looked like white, congealed foam. The bowl was placed in the center of the table. Her parents joined in with gathering more plates, knifes and such, as rice and peas were spooned out to form a bed of food on each plate.

"Time for the human!" Renee said with excitement in her voice.

"Cameron, we understand if this isn't what you're used to. Not everyone eats this, we know. Feel free to let us know if you don't like it," Vivianna told me with a grin.

Struggling for words, I began to sputter out words when Renee spoke again.

"Hummus isn't for everyone. We were pretty much grown before we could stomach Greek food."

"Hummus?"

"Oh yeah, I still remember the first time we had it. Viv was just a little kid. We went to this Greek place, and she looked at the menu and started to cry. She kept saying, 'Dad, I am not going to eat human!' over and over again. See, she saw hummus and thought it said human, she was really convinced that it was..." But Casper could no longer speak through his laughter. Renee slapped his arm gently.

"Cas, you're going to embarrass her again! First with the stupid bird, now telling baby stories, and you know she likes Cameron... Oops! Sorry, Viv."

"Oh, mom..." Vivianna looked at me with an expression of shyness. "Secret's out now, I guess."

We ate, I laughed and relaxed a bit.

"We like you too, Cameron. You really stood up for our daughter, and that means a lot. We wish people had stood up for us back in Austin, but it's good to know that bold people still exist."

"In other words, Viv, we approve," Renee stated, causing her daughter's face to glow all the more.

"Shall we eat dessert?"

"Sounds good Casper. Tonight we're having Ben and Jerry!" said Renee.

Yeah, of course, ice cream, I thought to myself. All night they've been messing with me, from lamp shades to beef jerky to Viv's odd way of saying hummus. I guess they wanted to get one more jab at me before dinner was over.

"You guys stay seated, I'll go and get it. Fridge is right in there, I guess?"

The family nodded. Yeah, Ben and Jerry, maybe that was the kids that were picking on her at school. In fact, come to think of it, Benjamin and Gerald, wasn't that... No, no more games.

I walked into the kitchen to get the ice cream when suddenly there was a shrill scream from the dining room. This scream was followed by the loud voice of Casper.

"Viv, get upstairs, Renee, call the police!"

Oh crap, I forgot all about the Tupperware. Mom must have packed one of her specialties. Damn it, mom!

The cops came and put me in this cage that I now write from. I would call my mom to come and help me out, but I have a feeling she's probably locked up in a similar cell as my own.

As weird as Viv's family was, I'm really disappointed that they reacted the way they did to the dish I brought.

Maybe it's mom's fault for leaving the wedding ring on one of them, but still, you'd swear Viv's family had never heard of finger sandwiches.

The Doctor and the Coffin Song

K. Banning Kellum

When the words become distorted it's best not to listen too hard.

Prentiss Dires was worried and his wife Rebecca could tell. She could read the man like a book, which made sense considering that they'd been married for almost 30 years. They'd met young, when Prentiss himself was fresh out of medical school. He'd taken some time off to travel and had found himself in Dublin, Ireland. There he'd met Rebecca McGillis. The story of their bonding, romance and eventual marriage is not something worthy of retelling. It was soft, clean and standard. Two young people locked in by mutual attraction. Rebecca, the charming Irish lass, Prentiss, the motivated newly minted doctor, it was rather mathematical and from that equation came a shared life of marriage and two children.

They'd had two girls, Shannon and Amy. Amy was doing well still, a young woman just beginning to find her way into the real world. She'd recently moved out of her parents' home in Kenner, Louisiana, and found a place of her own out in New Orleans East. She'd started dating a young man who Rebecca Dires adored and Prentiss thought was a bit of a slacker. A young guy that worked at a mall in a video game store whose name Prentiss always forgot. This drove Amy to annoyance as she was sure her father was doing this on purpose. In all truth, he wasn't, he just had too much on his mind lately.

The other daughter, Shannon, had departed not only the Dires home, but also life itself. She had fallen victim to a local string of serial killings a couple years before. The political murders as they'd been called in the news. The man responsible had turned himself in though and was currently spending the rest of his miserable life in a state hospital. He never confessed fully though, and Prentiss, using his connections in the medical field, kept tabs on the kid as he rotted away one day at a time out in Mandeville, LA, a ward of the Louisiana Department of Health and Hospitals now. Should he ever be declared sane, he would be commuted to prison. Prentiss was happy that the little freak named Craig Morgan had no chance of ever walking the streets again. It kept them all safer, because Prentiss had sworn to all the Saints above, that should Morgan ever breathe in the air of freedom, that he would personally find and kill the boy who took his daughter away from him.

That year, the year of Shannon's death, had been bad for the family, but none took it as hard as Prentiss. Rebecca was tough; her father, a huge redheaded Irishman who spent his entire life breaking his back working at shipyards had raised his daughter alone, and produced a strong and fearless woman. She took life as it came, head on and without apology. She mourned her daughter, comforted her husband and consoled her surviving child, but did all of this with a certain stoic power that Prentiss both envied and feared a bit.

Prentiss had been raised in New Orleans by a very traditional family in the part of town known as Gentilly. One could almost say his family was of the stereotypical New Orleans stock. Both Catholics, Mass attended every Sunday, no meat eaten on any Friday, whether it be Lent or not. They took trips to the lake, voted often, attended every parade and even rode in the Rex parade on Fat Tuesday each and every year. Prentiss had grown up happy and loved, but often wished he'd had a parent like Rebecca's, a man to instill that strength in him as her father had done for her.

"Life goes on, and so must we," his wife would tell him when he found himself in a bad spot thinking about their fallen daughter.

"She was so young though, just starting college, all the potential in the world. She was such a fighter, how could this have happened? What did we do to deserve this?" he'd reply, fighting back tears.

"God always has a plan Prent, you know that as well as I do. Why question it anyway? It's not like we'll know until we are called up ourselves."

Little exchanges like that had carried Prentiss slowly but surely through that horrible year that Shannon had been killed. Rebecca comforted him, but there was also a side of her that pushed him towards his own recovery. She was happy to hold his hand through it, but not while standing still. To take her hand, as her husband had learned years ago, was to be led, not to be coddled and allowed to wallow in pity. She had dragged him, as well as their other daughter Amy when she was feeling particularly distraught over the loss of her sister, through that dark time and finally back into a place that resembled the lives they'd known before their oldest child was taken away.

Prentiss had returned to his practice, Psychiatry, slowly. He cut his patient load in half, not wanting his own pain to reflect back towards those that came to him looking for answers and help. He had to take it his own way, and his wife supported that. One or two patients a day, three days a week was about the pace he'd started back at. Most of his returning patients were thrilled that he'd come back to medicine. He was a good doctor, so they all said, a man that cared. He actually found himself happy to be back at work again though he didn't want to admit that out loud. Part of him felt that he was almost disrespecting his deceased child by going back into the normal grind of life. For those moments though, he had Rebecca to bring him back to reality with her stern, yet loving Irish philosophy on living and dying.

Things had been going pretty well for him actually, and sometimes he would catch himself whistling as he walked to or from his car. Sometimes he'd get home, eat dinner, watch a movie with Rebecca, and not realize until they were in bed at the end of the day that he'd gone from sunup to sundown without thinking of Shannon once. He'd feel a bite of harsh shame at that sometimes. On nights when this shame kept him awake, he'd nudge Rebecca awake. She always knew what was wrong before she even rubbed the sleep out of her eyes.

"You're just living again Prentiss, 'tis nothing to be ashamed of. Shannon wouldn't want you to go out there and join her in the ground, now would she? Of course not! You're doing what any loving child would want their dad to do, surviving and living."

She was his rock in these situations, and as time marched on, her words rang true. He was allowing himself to be happy again. This was his own advice that he often gave to his patients; "Allow yourself to be happy, give yourself permission to smile. Sometimes what keeps us down and buried in our worries is the fact that we as people feel that we are required to suffer for some reason or another. We're not. Choose to feel something good today, grant yourself that much." His own words rang in his mind frequently and had been working well for sometime.

However, things had become different with the arrival of his latest patient. He started to worry again. Rebecca could tell just from looking at her husband that things were slipping backwards. He was consumed with something, and she decided to pull it out of him.

"Prent, if your face gets any longer tonight, I'm going to slap a saddle on your back and rent you out to pull produce," she'd said in a flat and strong voice. "Tell your better half what is eating you up so tonight."

"It's… a patient of mine. She was supposed to come in today. I know it's still early, but I called her and left a message, I thought I'd hear from her by now. False hope I guess. She'll probably call me late, once I'm already getting in bed or something. Then I'll feel relieved and will look much less like a horse. I'm just, getting worried. I think she might do something drastic. I wish I could do more, but… this is all I can do, sit and wait."

It wasn't uncommon for patients to call the Dires home to speak with their doctor. Sometimes it was just for some sagely advice, other times it was when the more pill happy members of the good doctor's practice would burn through all of their medication way too quick and call in desperate hope for a refill. Tonight though, it seemed different.

"Okay then, I know you got that oath and all, so I won't force you to tell me what is going on, but if you were to decide to empty your burdens, I wouldn't run off and tattle on you," she answered.

That didn't worry Prentiss. Oath or not, he'd shared details of some of his more extreme patients with his wife before. Maybe it wasn't the most prudent course of action for a doctor sworn to listen and heal minds, but it helped keep Prentiss on the right side of the couch he kept in his office.

"Coffee, then come and sit with me Rebecca. I will tell you, I have to tell someone after all."

"Oh, so now I'm your coffee wench am I?" she replied sarcastically, but filled his request just the same. She wanted him to talk so perhaps he could feel better, she was also a bit curious. Some of his stories about his patients were outright entertaining, and Rebecca, though she would never admit it, enjoyed hearing them from time to time. She had to fight not to laugh at some of them, like this one girl that Prentiss had treated a while back that needed her mother to call and sing her a lullaby every night. Rebecca had grown up with no mother and only her hard case dad and found such sentiments as lullabies to be almost laughable. She had a feeling though that this particular patient, the one keeping her husband awake and stressed, might not be such a funny story.

Prentiss took his cup, blew on some steam and brought it to his lips.

"Hey, slow down, it's hot dummy! You're going to burn your lips," his wife scolded. Her husband laughed and thought for just a moment that wives and mothers were not very different at all.

"Her name is Mary. She showed up at my office a few weeks ago, pretty standard stuff. Said that she was suffering from extreme anxiety. She's 35 years old, seems like she has a good head on her shoulders. I figured at first it was just the usual stress story; too much work, not enough money, you know, the usual. However, she was anything but the standard patient."

"How so?" Rebecca asked.

“Well, on paper she seemed like the least likely candidate to suffer from her level of anxiety. She had no children, a steady job in a rather low stress field. She’d inherited her home from her grandparents so she didn’t have a mortgage to worry over. As I said, on paper she seemed to be ahead of the power-curve in life. A lot of my patients would envy her situation, but I could tell after our first session that there was something very wrong going on. She had this.... Delusion you see, going all the way back to her childhood.”

Rebecca twirled her fingers a bit, a habit that drove Prentiss crazy sometimes. It meant to hurry the story along and get the good part. Prentiss didn’t know how to articulate to his wife that there likely was no good part in this story at all.

“Okay fine. I’ve been treating her for a few weeks now, and she told me all about this incident, one that I feel to be very much imagined, a nightmare from her youth, but to her it’s a cold hard reality. Tonight, well, tonight... according to her, she’ll die.”

“Die?”

“Or be killed, depending on how you look at her side of it.”

Prentiss sipped his coffee and locked eyes with his wife. She was leaning over, her red locks falling over her green eyes. She was wearing a sleeveless shirt and her orange freckles were on full display. He traced them around her arms with his eyes, a habit he’d enjoyed from the first time he’d seen her naked, way back in Dublin over 25 years ago.

"They wrap around my shoulders and lead right to my tits, same as always Prentiss, now stop dragging it out and tell me about this woman who thinks tonight will be her last."

He sighed, sipped his coffee once more, and told his story.

"As I said, she came in like any other patient, off the street really, no referral, no previous provider or therapist, at least from her records. I know sometimes patients will just pick a name out of the phone book, and I assume that's how she wound up in my office, sitting on my couch."

Mary, an attractive woman in her 30's, no real life issues that the doctor could tell from reading her chart. However, it took less than five minutes for him to realize that she had some very serious problems.

She came in and took a seat, smiled at him, and then the horrible silence that Prentiss had come to hate fell over them. It wasn't easy to just break the ice for him with patients; that was one skill he'd never mastered. Doctors of the body had it easy in his mind, fix a broken bone, heal an organ, it was all pretty black and white to him. Issues of the mind though, well, they were harder, at least in his somewhat biased opinion. So, finding the right greeting to break the ice was never easy. It's not like he could just say, "Hey, so you're crazy, huh? Well, let's fix that!"

No, he had to engage them in conversation, edge them into it. He was already dreading that song and dance when his patient took the burden from his shoulders.

"I believe I'm going to die before the end of this month," she said quickly.

“Okay,” he’d replied slowly, taking out his pen and paper. “Why do you believe that?”

“01-30-17."

“As in January 30th of this year?”

“That’s the date he told me I’d die.”

“Alright Mary, tell me about it. Who told you that you’d die on the 30th?”

“I was just a child then, a happy little girl on vacation. My mother had taken me to Grenada, Mississippi, ever heard of it?”

Prentiss shook his head.

“It’s a tiny little town about 90 minutes from Memphis to the south, and about the same distance from Jackson. A little place with not much to do besides play outside and watch the train blow through town a few times a day but my mother loved it. We went about six times a year back then. My great-grandmother lived there. I called her Granny. See, my mom didn’t have a great relationship with her parents at all, so my actual grandmother was barely in my life, same for my grandfather, although they did leave me their home in their will, that’s where I live now.”

“It always goes back to the parents,” Prentiss thought to himself, and decided to start there.

"Well, my grandparents were very… old school I guess. Typical New Orleans snobs I suppose. My grandfather ran a business for years and had fallen into the belief that he and only he knew what was right and wrong in the world. They were religious, but not, in your face about it, if you know what I mean?"

Prentiss thought about his own parents and knew right away what she meant. He'd grown up with a similar male influence in his life. Perhaps he'd be able to form a working bond with this patient from just that coincidence.

"Well, my mother, Lynn, she was the wild and free spirited type. So you can imagine that didn't sit well with her father. She opened a dancing school on Downman Road, if you're familiar with that part of the city, you might have even seen it, though it was a very long time ago.

So, she was young and pretty and kept with all the social circles. She seemed to live off of coffee and cigarettes. I can still remember my grandfather lecturing her about how she was going to blow away in a strong wind. My grandmother, on the few times we did visit them, would always stack her plate with bear-sized portions. It was just a little passive-aggressive statement on her part I think. My mom would just pick at the food though, which of course frustrated her folks all the more."

"How was your relationship with your mother?" Dires asked, almost smiling at such a cliché psychiatric question. All he needed was a German accent and the scene would have been complete.

"My mom? We were great. Cancer took her away a little over a decade ago. My grandparents joined her shortly after. Hurricane Katrina took them both at the same time. My grandfather refused to vacate his home, refused to evacuate even though the news and everyone else said that remaining in the city was practically suicide. Their home flooded when the levy broke, they weren't able to get out."

"I'm very sorry to hear that," the doctor responded.

"Yeah, it was tough, even though we were never that close. It still hurt. They left me their home though, and we were able to gut it and repair it. I live there now. In a lot of ways I'm actually happy we had to gut it out and re-do everything. Close or not, I think it would be strange, depressing even, to live there without them, you know, with the house looking the way it had back when they were alive."

"And you said your mother died from cancer?"

"Yeah, it came on quick. By the time the doctors found it, it was too advanced. The only positive thing that came of it was that she and my grandparents got sort of close, you know, towards the end. They repaired some damage they'd done to each other emotionally."

"Your mother's lifestyle, is that what drove the wedge?"

"Oh yes, they hated it. I can still remember my grandfather calling her a whore one morning. They were spraying our apartment for bugs or something, so we had to spend the night at their place. We were having breakfast the next morning, and my grandfather started in about my father, the man that I never met. He believed that my mom just didn't want a husband to tie her down, so she intentionally kept my dad out of my life. That wasn't true though. The truth was that my mother didn't honestly know who my father was. This didn't help her relationship with her folks at all. They argued about it and that's when he suddenly called her a whore, told her that she should learn to keep her legs closed, get married and be a decent mother."

"That must have been difficult to witness. How old were you when his argument happened?"

"Around 8, and trust me, it got much worse. My mother lost it. She had been known to do that from time to time. She'd been hospitalized with anorexia once and I think she was taking anti-depressants. Her moods could swing fast, and my grandfather was a real pro at getting that reaction from her. That morning, he'd already pushed her into the red, and didn't seem as though he intended to stop."

"Who the hell is that girl's father anyway!" he demanded.

"I could read on her face, him calling me that girl, that had been a mistake. The truth is, I knew whom my father way, or at least I think. My mom, when she was running her dancing school, back when she was a single wild-child, had kept a few lovers. One was a married man, the father of one of her students. They'd had a brief yet intense affair. I saw a picture of him once, years later, on a night when I was pressing my mom harder than usual to know the identity of my dad. I wouldn't bet all my money on him being my father, but I'd bet some. His face, the resemblance was there. Just some quick picture my mom had snapped of him when he was turning around or something. The eyes and mouth, just like mine. I guess she didn't want to ruin his life or her reputation. I suppose I'll never really know, but my guess is that he and I share some space on the same family tree."

"How did she react?"

"She started grabbing all the breakfast plates that she could reach off the table and smashing them on the floor. Over and over again, leaving little dents in the linoleum. My grandmother just sat there with this look of almost comical shock on her face. Her mouth had formed into a perfect circle. Had I not already started crying, I might have started laughing. My grandfather however didn't freeze in surprise, but rather struck in anger."

"What did he do?"

"He slapped her, hard. Hard enough to knock her out of her seat and down on the floor. I freaked out, started screaming and grabbing at his arm. He pushed me down hard, and that's what stopped it all. He loved me, I know that much. Even though sometimes I think he left me his house just to spite my mother. They'd set the will up before her death, and I still think they did that just to get one last jab in at their daughter. But seeing me hit the floor, well, that sobered him from his rage right away. He picked me up and started covering my face in kisses, telling me how sorry he was. My mother got to her feet and grabbed me away from him. She pulled me out the door and to our car without looking back."

"What did you and your mother do then?"

"Same as always, we went to Grenada to see Granny," Mary replied.

"Granny was sweet, loving, always wearing a smile. She didn't judge my mother for her free spirited life. She in fact praised it.

She had an entire wall dedicated just to my mom. Pictures of her when she was a Majorette for the New Orleans Saints, pictures of her dancing with some old actor named Danny Kaye. I think that Granny sort of lived though my mom in a few ways. She was a lonely woman; her own husband had gone on to join St. Peter in the clouds years ago. My mother's stories enthralled her though, and I know my mom took solace in having one parental figure that didn't spend all their time trying to shame her."

"Sounds like she was quite a remarkable woman," Prentiss states with a smile.

"Oh she was. She always smiled; she had this warmth about her that was almost never seen in people. I remember she always wore this old nightgown, no matter the time of day. Meals on Wheels brought her breakfast, lunch and dinner, so I suppose she never had much of a reason to dress up. She lived in a small home out there in Grenada where she'd lived her entire life. She was my grandmother's mother. My grandmother had met my grandfather when she'd left Grenada to go to New Orleans to attend school. Granny though, she was special. My mom always said that she'd be made a saint one day if God knew what he was doing. She died in 1996 at the age of 90. She lived a full life and had few regrets. She brought out a side of my mother that I almost never got to see."

"How so?"

"My mother was hardened to a degree. She was a woman on the move. Work, men, hobbies, she ate these things in giant gulps. Anything she did was done with an intensity that was in contrast to her open minded free living. But when she got around Granny, I don't know, she became like a kid again herself. They would sit up for hours telling stories. She would brag on about my small accomplishments in school. You'd think I was out there winning Nobel Peace Prizes by the way she would talk me up, and Granny would just sit there and nod, smiling and joining in on the praise. I remember she had these long fingernails, clean though, not like crazy old lady nails, and I would flop my arm in her lap and she'd gently scratch up and down. It put me in a trance. My mom would laugh, stories would continue and general happiness was felt by all."

"Sounds wonderful," the doctor interjected.

"It was... was wonderful. For years we made a regular pilgrimage to Grenada. Spending time with Granny seemed to center my mother. Sometimes, when we got back to New Orleans, my mom and grandparents would actually get along for a while. Those were some of my favorite times too. I mean, I know I've sorted painted them to be judgmental, but there was also a wonderful loving side to them as well. The tension between them and their daughter sometimes muddied that, but when things were going well, they were good grandparents. They loved me, I never doubted that, and I do believe that they loved my mother. Maybe all the fighting was just their way of showing passion, I don't know."

"You said it was wonderful, what changed that?"

"Well, that Doctor Dires, is why I'm here. It happened in 1994, I was 12 years old. After the incident, I refused to go back to Grenada. When Granny died in 1996, I didn't attend the funeral. The whole family was there, minus me. I ran away from home, went and hid out at a friend's house. My mother must have found out that I was there, I think my friend's parents get wind that there was a teenage girl hiding in their kid's closet. They knew me though, and instead of calling the cops or freaking out, they just called my mother and told her I was safe. My mom and grandparents, along with some family that'd moved to Houston, and some that had moved to Atlanta all attended. I stayed hidden away in a closet. When my mother got back, she wasn't mad though. Maybe the funeral had just taken all the fight out of her, or maybe she understood why I didn't want to go. All I know is that life went on. She lied to my grandparents, told them I was out of town on a school trip or something. But yeah, after what happened in '94, that damned February night, I could never go back to Granny's house, hell, could never go back to Grenada again."

That was where the first session with Mary concluded. They were out of time and Prentiss had other patients to see. She promised that she would return the following week and finish the story. She said that she had to, because the 30th was fast approaching, and she was still convinced that she would die that night. He shook her hand and assured her that she still had lots of life to live. Mary smiled back, but Dires was almost struck into sadness at the small, melancholy smile that appeared on the young woman's face. It was a smile that said, 'thanks for the kind words, but we both know how this will end.'

Over the next week, Dires, struck by a strange curiosity, did some research on Mary's story. There was in fact a town called Grenada. He dug deeper, looking into family members of Mary's, and found that her mother, Lynn, had in fact owned a rather successful little school on Downman Road throughout the 70's and 80's. Jazzercise had come to town though and driven a good deal of her business away, which led to the closing of the school. The grandparents checked out as well, both having perished in Katrina and the great-grandmother, real name Phyllis, Granny to all others apparently, who'd died from natural causes in '96. If this was a case of delusion or severe anxiety, Mary was certainly wrapping the rest of the story in the cloth of reality. He found himself strangely eager to hear the rest of her story. This was a strange attachment that he was usually able to avoid, but throughout that week, his mind continued to visit ghostly characters from Mary's story. The liberated mother, the conservative grandparents, and apparently a kindly old matron named Granny all danced through the doctor's mind as the days melted away and he finally found himself sitting across from Mary in his office once more.

He greeted her again, this time without the dread of breaking the ice, and asked her how she was feeling about the end of the month approaching. He was hoping that her telling at least some of her story might help in shattering this delusion of hers. He'd also researched some drugs that he thought might help and was going to offer them at the end of today's session.

"I have to tell you this before the 30th, before I'm gone," she began, and Dires felt a flush of disappointment that she was still living under this illusion that her life was counting down by the day. Without further small talk, she dove right back into her story. Dires wouldn't admit it then, but he was actually a bit thrilled to get back to the tale. Real or not, he was dying to hear the rest.

"February of '94, we'd gone on what I thought was just another routine visit to Granny. I was out of school for Mardi Gras break, a week off without much to do. We got there and things went the usual route. My mom and Granny swapped stories and caught up on what was happening in their lives since the last visit, you know, normal conversation. What was a bit different was that kids in Grenada don't get a week off for Mardi Gras, that's a New Orleans thing, as you well know. So, the kids that I usually would play with in Granny's neighborhood were all in school. What made things worse was that Grenada had a fairly aggressive truancy program. Kids seen around town on a school day were reported. I actually went out to play on my first day there.

Granny gave me a few dollars and asked me to run up to the grocery store around the corner from her house. Not thinking anything about it, I did as I was asked, and wound up being stopped by a cop at the store. I tried to tell him that I was on vacation from school, but he didn't believe it. He took me back to Granny's house to get the whole story, and it wasn't until my mother explained everything, even having to show her driver's license proving that we were from New Orleans, that he finally left. After that, I was sort of housebound, at least during the day.

My mom on the other hand ended up running into some old friends in town, some people she'd known when she was younger and would come here to visit Granny. They had made fast plans to go out for drinks or something, which left me locked in the house. This wasn't really a problem, Granny, and I were close after all, and we spent that afternoon telling stories and bonding all the more. I really wasn't disappointed about being left behind. At least, not until it got dark."

"What happened then?" Prentiss asked.

"My mother's little date or whatever ran way late. I guess she ended up having too much to drink or just having too much fun. She called from some bar and told Granny that she's be home very late, maybe even in the morning. I figured that she must have found a friend. Granny didn't judge though, just told her to have a good time and be safe."

"What happened that night?"

"The music got weird," was Mary's only response. Her tone of voice though, and the over all oddness of the comment caused goose bumps to run down the doctor's arms.

"I was bored, I won't lie. I loved Granny, but I was a 12-year-old kid. There just wasn't that much to do after all the little stories were told. Granny didn't have cable television, having to rely on the old rabbit-ears antenna to get a few fuzzy stations. Plus, she liked country music, I mean; she did live out in the country, and would often keep the television tuned into whatever channels played those old country programs. Her favorite was this show called Hee-Haw, ever hear of it; it was sort of like Saturday Night Live meets Mama's Family. She loved it though, and would laugh so hard that sometimes I worried she might break a blood vessel in her brain. That's what she was watching that night when things started to get scary. It was dark out by now and I knew my mom well enough to know she wasn't coming home anytime soon. Due to Granny's advanced age, she had the television turned up loud. I was trying to read some book or something, but just couldn't find the means to focus. So, I grabbed my book and politely informed Granny that I would take it to the bedroom.

The room that my mother and I slept in when we visited was in the back of the house. It was far enough from the living room to muffle a good deal of the television, but not far enough to drown it out altogether. The room was small and barely decorated, just a bed and a bunch of antique looking junk stacked up almost to the ceiling. I shut the door and sat down on the bed. There was no ceiling light in the room, only a lamp which cast a strange glow on everything. The room didn't exactly scare me, but there was always this sense of... I don't know, distraction in there. It was like my mind was constantly letting me know I was far from home and alone. Without my mom in there it really did feel distant, more so than usual. I tried to take solace in my book. I'd started reading it back at home and having those characters and settings visit me out here sort of brought me back to reality. Still, I felt an unease that simply wouldn't pass. I told myself that it was just because my mom was away and I was bored."

"Did that help?"

"No, the creepy feeling wouldn't pass. Finally I decided to just try to go to sleep. It was still early, but I figured if I could doze off, it would help pass the time until my mom got back. Then I'd feel all right again.

So, I turned off the lamp and closed my eyes. That damned television though, Granny still had it blasting out country themed comedy and now that my body was adjusting to the dark, it seemed as though I could hear every word, just with that muffled effect as the noise drifted through the walls.

I could tell that the show was thankfully almost over. I remember that at the end of every episode there would be a musical guest, some country singer or another of course. I was just laying there in the bed, listening as the familiar twang of the guitar started up, hoping that Granny would take the end of her show as a cue to go on to bed herself, or at least give the television a rest, when the singer started up. I remember it was a male voice, and he was singing something low and soft, a love song for sure. I could only hear every other word at first, but as my ears sharpened to listen, more of the song started became audible.

There was something doctor, something about his voice, or maybe the guitar twang, combined with being alone in that small, dark room, hundreds of miles from home, that began to make me nervous. Once I began to piece together the words, my nerves began to contort into a dread. It was strange, the trigger of the dread being something as simple as a muffled country song, but the sense of danger and well, wrongness, about what I could hear continued to grow. I began to latch on to the lyrics of the song. I didn't want to, but it seemed as though I couldn't stop myself."

Dires looked up from his notes and was a bit startled at the expression on Mary's face. She'd gone pale, her eyes staring directly ahead, not making eye contact but seeming to focus on the wall behind him. She was rocking slightly back and forth.

"What in the song lyrics frightened you so much?" he asked, a hint of hesitation in his voice.

Without speaking further, Mary surprised him as she began to sing. Her own voice, one that had been vibrant, took on a dead tone. "This is how a corpse might sing..." ran through Dires' mind, and he was shocked at how uneasy he felt, even in the safety of his own office in the middle of uptown New Orleans.

She began, singing in that sad, dead tone:
"Time runs up, life runs out,
But I'll always come for you,
There is no light at the end of the path,
Just a dark and lonesome view.
But do not be afraid when the trumpet plays,
For you won't die alone,
I'll come knocking on your door,
And I will take you home.
Because I'll put you in my coffin,
And take you home with me,
I'll put you in my coffin,
No light and you can't breathe,
But I'll put you in my coffin,
And take you home with me,
Your loved ones cry,
All life dies,
But I'll take you home with me."

Mary took a deep breath and stopped singing. Prentiss was grateful as he wasn't sure he could have taken much more. He asked her,"So, that happened when you were 12, and you remember all the words?"

"I'd hear it once more, the next night. Trust me, I didn't want to remember them, but it stuck in my brain."

"So what did you do, after the music?"

"I ran out to the living room, tears pouring down my face. I was terrified. Granny was out there, sitting in her chair. She'd just turned the television off. I asked her what that song was why the man was singing about putting someone in a coffin. I wanted to know why a comedy show would play something so horrible."

"And?"

"Granny laughed and hugged me, pulling me into her lap. She told me that there was no song about a coffin that the closing song was a duet between a man and a woman. No solo act, no coffin, and no death. She told me that I just had a bad dream."

"How did you respond?"

"I chose to believe her. She was Granny after all, a woman that didn't lie. She was the sweetest person in the world as far as I knew, and if she said I imagined it, I was more than willing to believe that. Still, I couldn't shake the feeling of dread and fear. Granny let me sleep in her room with her that night. I felt better, having someone with me, not being alone in the dark. However, I slept horribly. I kept thinking about that song, the words that I knew I heard. I wanted so badly to just go along with the idea that it'd all been in my head, but I couldn't accept it all together. I would be afraid until my mother came back. Hell, I might be afraid until we drove out of Grenada with the car pointed towards home."

"I can understand that feeling, being young and in an unfamiliar place, it can bring about fear in all of us," Prentiss replied, and was secretly happy that Mary had returned to her normal demeanor and was no longer staring forward with such intense emptiness.

Mary resumed, "The next day wasn't better. We woke up early and Granny cooked breakfast. No sign of mom. Granny asked me if I'd had any nightmares from the incident the night before. I lied and told her that I slept just fine. Breakfast was served, we ate, and I tried to make small talk with her as we did."

About an hour after breakfast, the phone rang. It was my mother, calling to tell me that she wouldn't be back until late tonight. I still remember how angry I was, really one of the few times I'd ever been that pissed at her. She explained:

"Baby, I'm all the way in Duck Hill. After we got back to Lloyd's place last night, some of his old friends called up and invited us out there. Lloyd started making phone calls and pretty soon it was a whole get together. We drove out there last night and honestly I just woke up. My car is back in Grenada and Lloyd has plans that he dragged me into all day, so by the time we get back to the car, it'll be late."

"I sat there, holding the phone and feeling anger build. Something worse too, a feeling more like betrayal followed behind it. She'd left me here with Granny, nothing to do but be terrified by songs in the middle of the night, while she was out having a good time. I wanted to be angrier, I wanted to tell her to come and get me right now, that I was more important that some guy named Lloyd and whatever foolishness he had cooked up out in Duck Hill, Mississippi. I wanted to tell her more, that I was scared, that something had happened last night and I really didn't want to be alone with just Granny.

But then I thought about how her parents treated her, how they always tried to make her feel ashamed about everything she did, and I let it go. I stressed that she come home as soon as she could, to which she agreed to try, and we hung up. Granny was looking at me, a knowing gaze in her eyes."

"Lynn staying out late tonight too?" she asked me.

"Yeah, hanging out with old friends or something," I had replied, trying to sound less distressed than I was. I didn't want to hurt her feelings.

"It's okay dear, we can pass the day together. It's nice to have company after all, normally it's just me and them," she replied distantly, and the strange comment honestly came so quickly that it was almost missed.

"Wait, you and who?" I asked her.

"Well, there's one in the attic, he's mean. Two of them live out back, mean too, but they're more likely to bite you and be done than sit on your chest all night trying to give you a heart attack."

"Granny, what are you talking about?" I demanded, scared now.

"Talking about what dear?"

"I looked at her, not quite sure what to say, she was just staring back at me, confused. I repeated what she said, about something in the attic and two things in the backyard. She told me that I must have heard her wrong. But I heard what I heard, and her voice was different now too, although I couldn't quite articulate what was different about it. Deader, that's the word that popped in my mind, although it made no sense to me. I decided I needed some time outside, in the sun. I was too creeped out now to stay inside with her alone."

"So, what did you do for the rest of that day?" the doctor asked.

"Stayed close to the house, but outside, in the daylight. I didn't want the cops to drag me back there again, but I needed to be out in the light and the air. I kept away from the backyard though. After all, Granny had said two of something that likes to bite lived back there. I didn't believe it, I'd been in that backyard the day before and saw nothing, but still, the way she said it, the tone of her voice, I was too scared to go back there. I kept praying that my mom would just pull up. I wanted to tell her about the weird song and Granny's strange behavior, but I knew my mom well enough to know I wouldn't see her until tonight… hopefully before I had to go to bed. When it started to get late, and I became too hungry to keep pacing around the front yard, I finally gave in and went back inside. I was hoping that whatever strange notions had come over Granny earlier that day had long passed."

"Had they?"

"I thought so, at first. I went back inside and Granny had dinner cooking. It smelled great and my stomach began to growl. Granny had that usual kind smile on her face. She asked me where I'd been all day. I told her I was out playing. She grinned at that and mused on the energy of youth. She served salmon patties, something I used to love, but can't really stand anymore. I remember I used to drown them in ketchup. She was telling me about how she'd learned the recipe and everything seemed normal. For the entire meal it was as if the night before and the strange conversation from this morning never happened, so, towards the end of the meal, I risked asking her about it."

"You asked her directly, about the comments?" Prentiss inquired.

"Yeah, and that was when things got weird again, but not just weird, mean."

"What happened?"

"When I asked her about the comments she made, about something in the attic, I still remember her reply. Granny had said:

"I get spells sometimes dear, just a part of getting old. We all get spells I guess, good ones and bad ones. Mine might be saying something strange that I can't remember. Yours might be hearing things that aren't there. Your mother's might be transforming into a whore at the first sight of cock and liquor."

"I honestly thought I hadn't heard that part. I would have never believed that Granny even knew such words, let alone would spin them into a sentence directed at her granddaughter, yet there it was. I looked back at her, my eyes wide, and could only muster enough to request that she repeat herself. Sadly, she did, she'd said:

"A whore dear, a dirty little whore, that's what she is. Put so much shame on us all, but that's okay, God punishes as well as rewards."

"How did that make you feel, her saying such harsh things?" Dires asked.

"I can't explain how it made me feel. I wanted to be furious at her, but this was Granny. I'd never felt anything but love and affection towards her. Even now, even with the nasty things she was saying about my mom, I couldn't quite mold anything into one emotion. I wanted to run out the door, but Granny had already applied the dead bolt. It was one of those that required a key both on the outside and inside. I was locked in. She still just sat there, smiling, as ketchup dried on her chin. It was like she didn't even register how terrible the things she'd said were. She kept on going too and began to speak even stranger things. She'd said:

"The things in the backyard, they like her. Always have. When she was a little girl, and she'd come here to visit, I had to do everything I could to keep them from coming inside. They wanted to see her up close. Normally they just hide back there, only biting if you get too close. They listen when you tell them to stay away though. The one in the attic though that one hates her. It's a wonder that it's never come down and visited her all the nights that she's stayed here. Awful thing to see up close, especially when it presses its face right into mine; it's a wonder my heart hasn't frozen in place by now. Maybe it will be nicer to you though."

"I demanded that she tell me what she meant. I wanted to know what these things were. I still wanted to know why she said such mean things about my mom. Granny though ignored my questions and simply smiled again, raising one crooked finger towards the corner of the living room."

"Oh look dear, there's one now," she'd told me, and began to cackle.

"I turned to look, but saw nothing. However, at that moment there was an enormous slam that shook the entire house. I felt that, I'd never forget it. The lights blinked for a moment, the chimes in the old clock rang a little, and I freaked out a lot. I shot from the table and tried the front door, anyway. I pulled on the knob, knowing full well that Granny had turned the bolt. I remember looking back at her and seeing her just rocking back and forth, laughing in that shrill voice. With no other options, I ran for the bedroom. I slammed the door and locked it. Like a scared child I hid under the covers and waited. All I wanted was my mother to come back. I would beg for us to go back to New Orleans if I had to, beg on my knees. I just wanted out of Granny's house, out of Grenada and far away from this insanity."

"Are you alright, do you need to take a break?" Dires asked Mary.

"No, we're almost done. I need to finish this. I don't want to die having kept this inside of me," she replied.

Dires was no longer sure that he wanted to hear this story. Everything about Mary had changed. Her voice had gone back to that dead tone, her eyes were now distant and didn't appear to be returning anytime soon. When she did the voice of the great-grandmother, she spoke in a voice that could only be described as an old witch. It sounded more frightening than it should be coming from a young woman such as Mary, yet Prentiss couldn't deny the fact that he was suddenly very uncomfortable. He'd never been afraid of a patient before, but he was starting to think there was a first time for everything. Still though, he was a doctor, a healer, and had a job to do. If hearing this young woman's story was the path to helping her, he'd see it through. He motioned for her to continue.

"I think I fell asleep, hiding there under the covers. I must have, because when I pulled the blanket off of my head, it was full dark outside. What was worse was that I woke up to the sound of the television, to the twang of a country guitar. The voice accompanying that guitar was familiar. I'd heard it last night."

"Please don't sing again," Prentiss thought to himself, but it was too late, she started once again.
"Because I'll put you in my coffin,

And take you home with me,

I'll put you in my coffin,
No light and you can't breathe,
But I'll put you in my coffin,
And take you home with me,
Your loved ones cry,
All life dies,
But I'll take you home with me."

She sang only the refrain this time, but to Prentiss that was not a relief. She was staring directly at him now, singing and rocking. Her eyes were dead; her voice was dry and devoid of life. Her eyes were burning into him. Finally, after repeating the chorus several times, she resumed her story. Her voice and eyes remained fixed and lifeless though.

"I ran out to the living room. I was going to unplug the television, or maybe smash the damned thing, I wasn't sure. I just couldn't take that song anymore. When I made it out into the dim light at the end of the hallway, I saw that the T.V. was already off. Granny was sitting at the dining room table, staring ahead, smiling. I looked right at her and demanded to know what the song was about why it kept playing every night. I half expected her to tell me that I'd imagined it again, I wish she had doctor, but instead she confirmed my terror."

She'd said:

"Dear, that's the song you hear when he has picked your numbers. Why, I still remember when he picked mine, 12-16-1996. Oh dear me, or should I say, oh dead me! I told him not to bother your grandmother or mother with theirs, just to give them to me, that I would bear that cross. It's not easy. He wouldn't just let me though, he said that was a lot to keep in one old lady's head, that's why he left his friends here, to keep an eye on me I guess. I sure wish they'd just watch though, the biting and scratching is rough on one such as myself. They get restless though, such as we all do."

"What are you talking about?!?" I screamed at her.

"Well now, ask him yourself Mary. See, I can't just keep holding on to all these numbers, it's too much for an old gal like me. So, have your own, I need a break."

"I opened my mouth to reply, to ask more questions, when suddenly there was a loud, aggressive and angry slamming on the door. I jerked my head in that direction doctor, looking to see. Through the window in the living room I could see headlights. The banging on the door grew louder. I started to cry. I wanted to run but my legs didn't want to work. That's when Granny called for him to come in. I looked at her, anguish and terror in my eyes, but she only smiled, as though she were excited to have company."

Just then the small clock that Dires kept on his desk chimed that the hour was up. The clock caused the doctor to startle from his seat. Mary continued though, and Dires was fine with allowing it. He wanted this over with; he wanted her to go so that this apprehension that had worked itself into his belly could fade. He'd work on a treatment, sure, but he could do without ever hearing this story again. She went on:

"The door flew open. I'm not sure if Granny had taken the lock off or not, but it was open now. Standing there was a man that looked insane. That's the only way I could describe him. His clothing was normal enough, dress clothes, church clothes I guess you'd call them. He wore a flat brimmed hat that covered much of his face. He was gaunt; he looked like he hadn't eaten in days. From what I could see of his facial features, he looked old. He raised his head just enough for his eyes to peek out from below his hat. Evil, that's all I could think. His eyes were evil. I don't remember the color or anything specific, I just know that if I'd had to look at them for more than a moment, I might have died of fright. He was humming, humming that damned coffin song. I wanted to be anywhere but in that living room, but my legs were still frozen. The old man walked in another step and began to speak in a voice that was old yet powerful, mournful yet full of fervor:

"01-30-2017.... 01-30-2017... 01-30-2017..."

"He repeated this over and over again. I couldn't take it. I turned to Granny, silently praying that she would grant me the peace and safety that she had always represented before this damned trip. I screamed at her, begging to know what he meant, why was he saying these numbers over and over again? Granny simply smiled and stated in a warm voice,

"Dear, don't be scared, he's just telling you the day that you'll die."

"I couldn't take it anymore, I ran from the room back towards the bedroom. I slammed the door and as soon as I did I began to hear that horrible song again, this time it seemed to come from everywhere. I ran to the window and ripped the curtains down. My hands fumbled about the lock, but the window was old and the locking mechanism hadn't been used in probably close to a century. I couldn't get it to budge. That's when the pounding on the bedroom door began. I could hear him out there, in that hallway, repeating those numbers. Between loud bangs I'd hear the doorknob rattle. He was trying to get in. Lost in panic and with no other options, I picked up the closest sturdy object I could find, in this case, a book, and smashed the window. It broke, and I climbed through. The glass cut my arms and legs a little, but in that moment I didn't care. Once I was out in the front yard, I saw the old man's car, what had been shining through the window earlier. It was a huge old car, black. From inside I could hear the radio, and of course it was playing that song.

I couldn't process anymore of this. I ran down the street, screaming for help through tears. I rounded a curve in the street and threw my head back once. The old man wasn't chasing me. When I turned forward, I was suddenly blinded by headlights directly in front of me. I dropped to me knees and covered my head with my arms. I was sure he'd come around and caught me somehow. That was when I heard the door of the car open and close and thankfully was greeted by the concerned voice of my mother. I looked up, filled with such relief. She was running towards me. I jumped into her arms, sobbing and begging her to take me home, to please just take me home. She was trying to calm me, trying to soothe me, and slowly, as the minutes ticked by and the safety of her arms and her voice began to calm me, I finally regained enough composure to tell her what had happened."

Dires put down his notes and was relieved to see that some old Mary had returned. That distant stare was gone and her face had regained some color.

"Against all of my screaming, terror-filled protests, we went back to Granny's. There was no black car in the front yard. The broken window remained however. Once inside, my mother began to pelt Granny with questions. I'd told her everything, even the terrible things she'd said about her. And you know what doctor; Granny didn't seem to recall any of it. And part of me believed her because to accept any of what did happen would be to accept so much darkness with it. My mother talked to her for a long time that night, asked her over and over again if anything happened. Granny told a simple story of salmon patties and a tired out great-granddaughter who went to be early. Granny said that she'd fallen asleep and didn't even hear the glass break. In the end it was all determined to be a nightmare. My own mother bought into that. And for a long time so did I, after all, the nightmare version made far more sense than the story I told. I wanted to get back to normal and believing it was all just a bad dream seemed to do it. We spent one last night in Grenada, but we did so at a motel. I simply refused to spend another night in that house. The next morning we drove back to New Orleans, and I never returned to Grenada again."

Prentiss rubbed his chin and nodded. Now that the story was told, he felt a lot better. That sense of dread that had taken over him was fading to almost nothing now.

"So Mary, if you say you accepted it as a bad dream, why believe in it now?"

"The dates. Granny died on December 16th of '98, just as she said she would. Like I told you before, I didn't attend the funeral, but my mother did. She came home with some of Granny's personal items. A book was one of them. One day when I was home alone and bored, I decided to dig through some stuff. The book, a family bible, contained a list of three dates. It read:

Me: 12-16-98

Lynn: 04-11-04

Verna: 08-29-05

"Verna was my grandmother's name. Somehow Granny had been dead on with the dates for the deaths of her daughter and granddaughter. That was when I started to believe, and now my day is almost here."

Mary looked down, tears showing in her eyes. "I don't want to die Dr. Dires, I really don't."

"Then don't," he replied. "Choose to live. We will get through this together. I can refer you to a hospital if you'd like. Be somewhere with people on that date, I'm sure you'll feel better with people around you."

"It won't matter. My mother was in a hospital when her date came, fighting cancer. I think if it's going to happen no matter what. I just wanted to tell someone about it. I hate carrying this inside of me."

"I will not let you die Mary. I tell you what, come and see me on the 30th. In the mean time, I want you to try out this prescription. It should help with your anxiety, help you sleep better too. I think that once you make it through the 30th and see that you're still alive and well, you'll really be able to move forward."

Mary smiled, but it seemed to come from no place of joy. She took the prescription and tucked it into her purse. She shook Dires' hand and thanked him for listening.

"And today is the 30th, and let me guess Prentiss, she didn't show up," Rebecca asked.

"No, she was a no show. I called her number on record but got nothing but voicemail. I told her to call me. I've been sitting here debating calling the cops and having them go and check on her. Problem is, I don't believe she's suicidal, I think she just believes this bogeyman is going to show up or something. Calling the police would shatter any trust that I've built with her, especially if she simply got called into work or missed the appointment for some other mundane reason. I still want to treat her, I feel that there is more to do, but if I go and scare her off, she may never open up to me again."

Rebecca went over to the living room mantel and pulled down a small picture of Shannon. She was smiling, looking so alive and full of joy. Rebecca felt her stomach flip a bit with grief. She sat down next to her husband with the picture in hand.

"You can't save them all Prentiss, and you can't look at this Mary woman and see Shannon. If this woman wants to be helped, she will come back. Or perhaps you did help her, maybe she didn't show up because talking to you got her through it."

Prentiss looked at his wife and kissed her once on the corner of her mouth. "Thank you Rebecca, I think you might be right."

"Of course I'm right," she replied with a grin, and suddenly grabbed her husband by the hand. "Now come to the bedroom Prent, it's my turn to give you some therapy, let you trace those freckles a bit more."

Prentiss looked down at his phone once, decided that Mary wasn't going to call, and went to join his wife in their bed. When they were done, he found that he felt much better after all. Rebecca could cure most any problems he might have. He went over to get some ice water for his wife when he noticed the little blue light on his cell phone was flashing. Picking it up, he saw that he'd missed a call from Mary. He felt a bit of shame, he'd been busy screwing while a patient needed him, but he also saw the call came in just a short time ago. He opened his voicemail and listened to the message.

A few minutes later he came into his bedroom. Rebecca looked up, "Forgot my water I see, should have figured..." she stopped when she saw his face.

"My God Prentiss, what has you looking so?"

He sat down next to his wife and activated the speaker on his phone. Next he played the voicemail. He and Rebecca listened to it several times, not speaking, only staring down at the phone, mouths hanging slightly open with confusion. The recording played, Mary's familiar voice was distorted mostly in static, but the words that did come through chilled the doctor and his wife to their core:

".... it's dark..... no... air...... can't breathe.... doctor.... help..... the song.... no light.... please...."

The voicemail ended. Prentiss and his wife exchanged a look fear and concern. Mary's words were distressing, her gasps were terrifying, but the soft twang of a country guitar in the background left them both speechless.

The Funny Foul-Up of Frantic Falcone

K. Banning Kellum

It's not always a cause for celebration when the students become the teachers.

It was a normal Tuesday. I had taken the day off of work to bring my son in for a doctor's visit. I went to the same doctor's office that I had always brought him to. Just as routine, I sat down and waited for him to be called back. There was a selection of books, most of them for kids, sitting on the little desk next to our seats. I reached over and looked through them, deciding to read him a story while we waited. Most were your average kid books. Then I found a new one, one I had never seen before. The cover was gone, ripped off by some other careless kid probably months ago. The condition of the book was poor at best. Since I didn't recognize the story, I decided to read it to my son, something new.

The cover was gone, as I said, by the first page of the book displayed the title, as well as a cover illustration. The book was called "The Funny Foul-Up of Frantic Falcone". It showed a man, probably in his early 40's, standing in front of a classroom of kids, probably 5th or 6th graders. The kids in the picture were all shouting and laughing, while Falcone, obviously the teacher was waving his arms around and trying to quiet them down.

The style and quality of the artwork suggested that this would be a run-of-the-mill kids book like the ones I grew up on. Oddly, I couldn't remember ever reading, or hearing about this one. So, I turned to this first page and began to read. You'll understand soon why I didn't read much past the first page to my son, but I did read the entire book for myself.

It opened with an illustration of Mr. Falcone walking up to a school.

"This is Mr. Falcone, a teacher. He teaches 6th graders. He has been a teacher for a very long time, almost fifteen years, and he used to love teaching kids."

Now, I found that weird from the start, why would the book say that he "used" to love teaching, doesn't he still? I read on.

"Nowadays, Mr. Falcone has to teach, even though he doesn't want to anymore. He has a lot of debt, and no family or friends to help him. If he doesn't work, the bank will take away his house. Mr. Falcone is sad."

Honestly, I thought this was funny. I figured maybe this was a book to teach kids about the evils of corporate greed, or to shine a light on the low wages of American educators. I turned the page.

The next page showed Falcone walk into his classroom. He is looking at the chalkboard where someone wrote "Falcone is a FREAK." I thought this was a little harsh for a kid's book, but I did stuff like that in the 6th grade, so maybe the author was trying for realism here.

"The children in Mr. Falcone's class are always telling him how they really feel about him, as they demonstrated on the chalk board. Poor Mr. Falcone."

The next page showed two of the kids in Falcone's class, which would turn out to be the only two kids shown in the book.

They were both drawn in that very real and detailed style. On the surface they looked like two normal kids, but after looking at their faces, I could see the artist put a lot of time and detail into really highlighting the contempt and hatred these two had for Falcone.

"Meet Charles and Joe. They hate Falcone almost as much as God hates him."

By this point I handed my son a coloring book. I wasn't sure where this particular book was heading, but I didn't need his mind getting warped either. Once it was only my eyes on the pages, I read on faster.

"Joe wants to be a dentist when he grows up, as you can see, he brought in some 'tools' to practice with today."

The next picture showed Falcone being held down and strapped into a dentist chair. Joe walked over with what looked like an old-fashioned doctors bag and took out a pair of pliers and a screwdriver.

"Time to practice!"

The next page was one of those hologram-style plastic deals that you could tilt to change the image. It showed Joe ripping out Falcone's teeth. Blood and teeth would fly across the room when you tilted the page. It was very graphic. This was no children's book.

"Look at all the blood, guess Joe still has a thing or two to learn before he becomes a dentist. He forgot to bring a suction!"

The next illustration was Falcone, staggering towards his desk. Charles steps out in front of him.

"Charles wants to be a soldier, or maybe a police officer when he grows up. See his combat boots? He shines them every day before class."

The following page was of Charles kicking Falcone in the crotch. The look of agony on the teacher's face was sickening. Someone put a lot of time into that. The look on Charles' face was of pure evil glee.

"Mr. Falcone teaches lots of lessons, but today, his students teach him a lesson in economics."

The illustration accompanying this was of Falcone discovering his pay check had been ripped to shreds and left on his desk. The next three pages are of Falcone simply sitting at his desk, his head in his hands, quivering. Tears can be seen forming puddles on his desk.

"Sharing is important. Charles is about to share one of his favorite devices with Mr. Falcone."

Charles is shown holding what appears to be a boxing glove attached to a trigger activated spring.

"Hey Mr. Falcone, here comes the PUNCH GLOVE!"

The device fires, and the glove strikes Falcone hard in the face. More blood can be seen, and his nose clearly breaks.

The next few pages are torn badly. In one it appears the kids are damaging Falcone's car. In another Falcone can be seen pleading with another adult, maybe the principal. Clearly it doesn't work as the next complete page shows him back in the classroom.

"School is almost over, so Mr. Falcone reaches for one of his few pleasures, his cigarettes. UH OH, looks like Charles and Joe wanted to show Mr. Falcone that smoking is bad for you."

This page shows Falcone holding up a pack of cigarettes, which are dripping with water, ruined.

The next page is Falcone taking the bus home, the page after that shows Falcone returning home to find that his house has been foreclosed.

On the second to last page, the illustration of Falcone is looking directly at the reader, his eyes are bloodshot, he is bruised and bloodied.

"Only one thing left to do," written across the bottom.

The final page shows Falcone blowing his brains out.

I threw the book in the trash. No child should accidentally pick that up and read such a horrible story. Clearly this was someone's morbid idea. After my son finished his appointment, I fished out the book and decided to see if I could find out who wrote it or published it. There was no author's name given, but I did find the address for the publishing company. I wrote them a strong letter, expressing how their book, clearly meant for adults, but written and illustrated in the style of children's books, had found its way into a pediatrician's office.

I never received a response, and as far as I can tell, the publishing company doesn't exist. I still wonder what their inspiration... or intent was behind publishing such a story. Furthermore, how many more books did they publish, and what lessons did those books try to teach?

The Unkillable Kenny Leonard

K. Banning Kellum

All writers struggle from time to time. Demons and cults though are only for the special ones!

The Office.exe

Lost in the archives of NBC, never viewed by the public, locked away for all time… The Office: Michael's Bad Day.

It began as most episodes did, with a soft opening featuring Jim Halpert pulling a prank on Dwight Schrute. Jim messed with something on Dwight's computer, which caused every website he attempted to open to direct him to a sex offender registry.

"Very funny Jim, what did you do to my computer?"

Jim looks at the camera and makes his trademark face, "Oh, the cops were in here earlier Dwight. They were doing something on your computer. They said you needed to register on some website or something and they set it up to auto-load so you could find it."

"Stop it Jim, I am not a sex offender!"

"Well, that's not what they're saying about you on the news."

"Damn it Jim," Dwight grunts with annoyance as he marches into the office of Regional Manager Michael Scott to lodge a complaint against his co-worker. Jim smiles and follows Dwight into the office and then both men can be seen stopping and looking concerned.

Michael Scott, usually a happy and goofy character is instead seen sitting slumped in his chair with his head in his hands. Soft weeping can be heard.

"Michael, what's the matter, who hurt you?" Dwight asked, showing concern laced with his typical bootlicking mentality.

"I don't want to live anymore," Michael responds, never looking up at the camera.

The episode then goes through the normal opening credits, however, the normal little song that played seemed... warped somehow. It was playing much slower and some parts of it seemed to play backwards. The overall lightning also seemed much darker. The ending of the credits though that's what really scared me. Instead of showing the little wooden office sign, it showed a tombstone. I have to admit, I wasn't sure what I was watching anymore. Why did I choose to download this off of a Russian torrent website? What was going on here?

The episode then opened, but it remained where the soft opening left off, with Dwight and Jim expressing concern for Michael Scott.

"Are you okay Michael?" Jim asks.

Slowly, Michael lifts his head, his eyes red from crying, and looks Jim in the eyes.

"No one came to my BBQ. I made sure everyone was off for the weekend, even went around and asked if anyone had plans. Everyone said they weren't doing anything. The I.T. guy checked your emails, and we didn't find any big RSVP's going on in there Jim!"

"Wait, you checked our emails?" Jim asks.

"Yes Jim, I checked your precious emails. So, I send out my invite for a huge gathering at my condo, and no one showed, not even you Dwight!"

"Sorry Michael, I had to castrate a horse and then my mother..."

"Not helping," Jim whispers, jabbing Dwight with his elbow.

"I am just so tired of being lonely..." Michael whispers and begins to cry again.

"We should go," Jim tells Dwight. The two men exit the office when suddenly Michael bursts through the door with a handgun raised in the air.

“I am just so tired of being lonely!” he screams, firing a shot through the ceiling. Other members of the office cringe and gasp as Michael Scott begins aiming the pistol towards his staff.

“Michael wait, I would have come to your BBQ, I never miss free food,” Kevin Malone, the obese accountant tries to explain, before Michael shoots him in the chest. The rest of the staff scream and begin to try to find an escape. The camera then cuts to one of those “talking head” segments, showing Kevin’s corpse propped up; a large gunshot wound oozing blood from the center of his chest.

The episode then cuts to black, but sadly doesn’t end. I could still hear people screaming as the voice of Michael Scott could be heard shouting about being lonely no more, then a gunshot. This repeated for about 10 minutes, just that black screen with the horrible sounds.

Finally, the episode resumes, showing Michael Scott sitting in his condo. The corpses or his co-workers are thrown about his living room, some sitting in chairs; others just tossed on the floor.

“I guess they don’t mind hanging out with me now!” Michael shouts towards the camera, his face alive with morbid insanity.

In the next scene...

“Okay, dude, stop, this fucking sucks!” my so-called best friend, Jason shouts through sarcastic laughter and possibly genuine annoyance.

"Wait, what... I'm not even done with it yet; there are still four more chapters. Michael Scott goes to New York next and confronts the corporate bosses for never giving him his proper respect, then he returns to deal with the bodies, it gets better!" I argued back.

"No Kenny, this is garbage. If you submit this, they're going to laugh you right out the front door. The Office, really, you think this is a good premise for a horror story?"

"I think it has potential," I tried to convince my friend and roommate, but I knew Jason well enough to know it was a lost cause.

"What else do you have?" he asked.

"Okay, I have this one I wrote about a secret ending in an old VHS copy of Ol' Yeller, you know, the story about the dog that goes rabid. See, in this one, he escapes and mauls the family and..."

"NEXT!" Jason shouted, still laughing.

"Fine, how about this, since I work at a used video game store and all, I wrote one where an old man comes in with a used copy of some NES game, but the label is missing and..."

"Oh Christ no... NEXT!" Jason screamed.

"Shit, okay, let me just pull this one up... here we go. It opens with: In any town or city, go to any video store or mall that is opened after 8pm and ask the clerk for the back room. He'll give you a sad look but hand you a key, take the key down a long hallway which wasn't there before..."

"Mercy Kenny, I beg you for mercy, no more shit stories tonight, I don't think I can take them anymore." Jason, always the performer, got down on his knees and mock pleaded with me. I felt like shit.

"Kenny, I don't know how to tell you this, but... well, you suck at writing horror."

He was right, I knew he was right, and it stung. I'd always loved horror, I'd watched just about every horror movie and read all the scary books from the time I was old enough to watch or read anything. I loved the genre. However, Jason did have a point, I was pretty lousy at this. All my ideas were either stupid, unoriginal or, as he loved to say time and time again, cliché. I swear that's Jason Holmes' favorite word folks, cliché. I felt like I was stuck in that episode of South Park, the one where the guy kept trying different schemes but it turned out The Simpsons had done them all before. Yeah, that's how I felt, Kenny Leonard, master of the shit story.

This went on the rest of that night. I would show Jason something else I'd written, which he would laugh at, or brainstorm a different idea, which he would also laugh at. This was becoming depressing. The ideas, like The Office story, seemed really crisp and original in my mind, but once they were laid out on digits, well, it just looked pathetic. Hey, like I said, I admit it, I can't write.

So why even try right? Okay, well, at the risk of sounding cliché, that fucking word, I was doing this to impress a girl. Yep, that's right Faithless Reader; this was all about a girl. Sounds like the start of some lame rom-com rather than a scary story, doesn't it?

So, fast-forward to right now, the present. I am sitting at the Good Grooves coffee shop in Pearl River. What a freaking little hick town this is folks, let me tell you. It's about an hour from New Orleans, and how I wound up here is a story almost too boring to be worth mentioning. But, I need something to do to kill the time until they call my name, so why not, here goes.

Jason, my shit ass roommate, and me both work at The Plaza, a giant mall in eastern New Orleans. I work at this hole called Gametrader, a little privately owned used game place. There are four of them in the city and one about to open out in the sticks, which is part of the reason why I am sitting in the weird little bohemian refuge in the middle of cousin-fucking territory. All will be explained though, oh Faithless Reader. Yeah, all 16 or you that read my blog, anyway.

So, I work as a manager at The Plaza location. The Gametrader out in the sticks, that's in a town called Bogalusa, Louisiana. Don't believe me, look it up. It has a paper factory and stinks like rotten eggs and cabbage half the time, but the owners, in their eternal brilliance, decided to put a new store out there. See, Gametrader is so small that as a manager I essentially report right to the owners themselves. It's cool I guess. I mean, I am a two-time community college dropout, and I doubt I will be able to convince my mom to send me back a third. Guess it's true that not all nerds are smart, right?

So, having a management job is actually pretty lucky for a guy like me. 22 years old, no real education outside of four very marginal years of high school. Gametrader pays enough for me to make my half of the bills each month, with enough cash left over to keep my World of Warcraft account going. Yeah, I know, my life is lame.

Anyway, a few nights ago, as I am getting ready to close up Gametrader and go home, one of the owners drops in. This wasn't too uncommon, like I said; we were a small company, and the owners were very hands on.

"Kenny, how's it going?" asks Jon the owner.

"It was a busy day Jon, made some good sales. I got us a copy of Final Fantasy 8, convinced the guy to trade it in for store credit."

Jon was pleased with that. This was usual banter between us. He liked when we bought expensive games off of people for crap like store credit. Typical mind set of the owners. Of course, Jon wasn't the one that had to get chewed out by said kid's parents later when they found out that I bought an $80.00 game off of some kid for $20.00 store credit. It didn't really bother me though. He was happy and therefore I was happy. Anyway, Jon was carrying a huge cardboard box full of random game stuff. Controllers from old systems like the NES and Sega Master System. Games galore of course, and other little accessories that only the most hardcore gamer might remember. He sat the box down and gave me this crooked little smile that I knew was going to translate to a pain in my ass.

"So, what's my favorite manager got planned for tonight?"

Great, nothing good ever follows when he refers to me as his favorite anything.

"Just going home to watch TV or something."

"Great, so you don't mind running these out to the new store tonight, do you?"

"As in Bogalusa? It's two hours away Jon, and it's already almost 9PM!"

"Yeah, those guys are working overnight out there, setting up the final touches on everything. We're doing a sort of grand opening tomorrow. I really want to have these old games and extra accessories out there so they can fill their rare case."

"It's kind of late though…" I was trying to argue back, but I knew he was going to keep pushing.

"Time and a half?"

Damn him. That would be a nice boost to my paycheck. I could probably afford this old Magic card I'd have my eyes on. Yes, I'm a nerd, we established that.

"Fine Jon, you got it."

He smiled and shook my hand. We shared a few more words before he headed on out, leaving the box of crap behind for me to truck out into the green country. I glanced into the box and found it much as I expected. Just a lot of gaming junk and accessories. Then something caught my eyes, an NES game that was missing the label. It looked old, and in place of the title, written in black marker were the words, "Death Game: Do Not Play." I simply couldn't help myself... okay, okay, just kidding folks. There was no missing label game, just a bunch of random NES and Sega games and controllers. Ha, creepy NES game, what a load.

After locking up the store and loading the box into the trunk of my car, I began the long journey from New Orleans to Bogalusa. Music helped a little. I tried to call a couple of people, the few friends that I had at the time, but no one was answering. The radio was just recycling the usual Top 20 garbage, and soon enough I turned it off and just listened to the silence of the surrounding road. I was passing over the Twin Span, a pair of bridges that extends over Lake Pontchartrain connecting New Orleans East to the small suburb of Slidell when the fatigue started setting in a bit. Now, I'm young enough to be able to hang in there, but still, the idea of driving on some super dark country roads with my eyes weighing me down didn't exactly appeal, so I decided that I would push on for a few more minutes and then find a place to buy some coffee.

Okay Faithless Reader, I guess it's only fair to admit that I am pretty dumb, as if my sample of stories I mentioned above aren't enough to demonstrate that. I must have passed half a dozen all night gas stations and never once pulled in. I kept on driving, exiting in Slidell and converting over to the smaller highway that would take me through Pearl River, out to some little dirt town called Bush and finally into Bogalusa. Maybe I exaggerated when I said it was 2 hours away, maybe more like an hour and a half, but still, I was getting sleepy and the darkness all around me wasn't helping. I had officially entered Pearl River, and from the looks of things, I was starting to think my coffee break would never happen. The whole town looked dark. Nothing out there but dirt roads and trees for miles. I was starting to think I should just turn around and go back to Slidell when I saw a sign up ahead.

Good Grooves Coffee House. Oh wow, if this joint was open I was saved. Hot java, good grooves, what else could a 22-year-old that managed a video game store ask for? A hot girlfriend perhaps? Who could have guessed, right?

Firstly, I was amazed that the place was open this late in a place like Pearl River. Not only was it open, but it seemed to be doing quite a bit of business as well. Cars were lined up in front of the place and also parked along the highway for a good distance. I found a place fairly close to park, locked up the car and trotted over. Looking through the glass walls from the outside, I could see the coffee shop was lively for almost 10PM in a town that seemed to go to bed around 7. Lots of young people, college types maybe, were sitting at tables, sipping coffee and chatting. I walked in, feeling that slight sting of social anxiety that comes standard with all nerdy types like myself, and that, oh Faithless Reader, is when I saw her.

Mid 20's, hair dyed pink on one side and blue on the other. She was wearing some anime shirt or another, a short skirt and some rather impressive moon boots. I think I died and went to nerd heaven. She was a geek's wet dream. She was standing behind a table that had been set up like a booth, and a couple of other folks, two girls and a guy, were standing around chatting with her.

I begged myself not to fall in love on the spot. Not real love, you know, infatuation I guess is the right word. Still, I couldn't leave this strange little late night coffee spot in the middle of nowhere without at least checking out the sign that she'd hung from her little table-booth she was standing behind. However, before I could even read it, she addressed me.

"Oh, we have another horror fan here I think?" she said to her three friends gathered around her.

I wanted to say something cool in response, but of course muttered something stupid. Girls like her made me stammer like a damned fool. I'm such a lucky guy.

"Horror, yeah, it's the meat to my life sandwich," I replied, and felt like a fucking idiot. To my amazement she actually laughed though.

"What's your name?" she asked me with what seemed legitimate interest.

"Kenny Leonard."

"I'm Tempest Avalon, and I'm hosting a little local horror writing challenge, as the sign says."

The sign did in fact confirm that the flirty little Tempest Avalon was running some sort of horror contest.

She continued, “There will be prizes for the top 3 stories. 3rd place gets a gift certificate for GameStop of something, 2nd prize is $200.00. First prize gets a date with me!”

I could tell she was trying to hold back laughter with the 1st place prize. It was probably a larger cash purse or something, but in all truth, I liked her suggestion better. In a strange moment of smooth confidence, I actually said something that didn’t sound like virginity pressed into a blender and poured into a dumpster.

“I want that prize, if you’re serious, I’ll write something that’ll make Stephen King shit his pants.”

Tempest’s friends rolled their eyes in the automatic pretension that likely follows them everywhere, but she was actually staring hard at me, a small grin on her face.

“Okay then Kenny, go for it. You win first prize and we’ll go out on a date.”

“Really?”

“Sure, why not? I can see by your t-shirt that you work at Gametrader. I guess if I could sleep with a professor for a good grade in psychology, I can sleep with you for a free copy of Chrono Trigger.”

I was struck silent. She broke that silence with more laughter.

“Kidding! About the sleeping around for a game, not the date though, I’ll honor that.”

Damn if this wasn't going well. Anytime a girl spoke to me for more than a few minutes was a win in my mind, but when she added on a potential night out, well damn, I mean... damn! I wanted to stick around and chat with her a while longer, but then I remembered the box of games that I had to get out to Bogalusa. She gave me a copy of the rules for the contest, the due date to turn in my story and a few other contest specifics. I bid her goodnight and left without even buying any coffee. I was plenty awake now.

I drove the rest of the way out to Bogalusa with a smile on my face and a strange energy burning inside me. Just like that my night went from running boring errands for my boss to potentially going out with a girl that was way too hot for me and apparently funny and into horror as well. I thought I was going to wake up any minute from some awesome dream.

The contest, now, that was simple enough. Write an original horror story; submit it to her by the following week and then show up Friday night when they'd announce the winners. She, along with her three friends that she referred to as the admins would be doing the judging. Too easy, right? After all, I'd been a horror fan since I was old enough to be a fan of anything. I'd seen hundreds of horror movies and was a regular at the infamous House of Shock haunted house every Halloween. I was pretty confident that I could put together something scary enough to win a coffee house horror contest. Write it, print it, and drop it off; three easy steps to win a date with a girl that I'd likely be afraid to speak to under any other circumstances. Good times, hell, good grooves.

The rest of the trip to and from Bogalusa went smoothly. With my mind on the lovely Tempest, I barely noticed the distance closing. I got to the new store, delivered the games, made some small talk and then was on my way back home. The entire ride back to New Orleans, I brainstormed different story ideas. Such gems as The Office lost episode story that I already mentioned came to mind. I decided that I'd go home and write a few of them and enlist my asshole friend and roomie to help me pick the one to submit. However, as you already know, he hated them all, and I had no clue what to do after that.

Over the next couple of days I just sort of went through the motions. Go to work, come home, try to write something, get made fun of by my roommate, try something else, fail, wash-rinse-repeat. That was the great story of Kenny Leonard: Horror Writer Extraordinaire. I sat in front of my computer for over an hour, trying my best to just get the first damn paragraph going on something that didn't come out terrible, but it seemed nothing I did was worth submitting. Then something happened. Maybe it was the miserable reflection of my face gazing back at me from my screen; maybe I was just sick of my friend making fun of me. It was like, in The Grinch movie, you remember that part where he grows a heart, well, I think I grew some balls. I decided, totally spur of the moment, that I'd ride out there to Good Grooves and just ask Tempest out on a real date. I'd tell her that I was too busy or something to write a worthwhile story, but that I really was interested in the date. I'd give her my phone number and just head on out the door. If she called, great, if not, well, I always had my level 85 Paladin in Warcraft to dry my tears.

The ride out to Pearl River was as boring and mundane as ever. I kept going over how I would ask her out in my head. I was preparing for rejection, but figured I'd likely never see her again, anyway. A moment of embarrassment and then I would be done trying to write some horror story that I clearly lacked the skill to accomplish. And who knows, maybe she would say yes. Double win, right?

Wrong, double lose. When I got there, the place was closed. Fucking Pearl River, damn hick town, who the hell closes the only coffee house at 8pm on a weeknight? Sure enough though, no cars were there, and the lights were all off. Great, I wasted gas and time to come out here for nothing. And that folks, is when I noticed the sign above the store. It no longer read Good Grooves. It now read: Pearl River Funeral Home-Established 1959. Had this place never been a funeral home all along? Had I...

Kidding!! Sorry Faithless Reader, I couldn't resist. No, the place was still Good Grooves; the sign on the door just confirmed that I'd decided to come out here on the one night of the week that they close early; lucky me, right? So, now I was out here, all-alone at night in the country with nothing to do. I honestly didn't want to go back home and deal with another night of my roommate making fun of my inability to generate a scary story. So, once again I made a spur-of-the-moment decision and decided to just ride out to Bush or Bogalusa, and then turn around and head back to New Orleans. I sort of found that I enjoyed driving through the country at night. There was a peace and silence to it that couldn't be found in the city. Plus, I had nothing better to do, so why not clear my head? Maybe I'd finally come up with that horror story and still win my date with Tempest. And maybe pigs will fly too; I mean, it could happen, right?

Okay Faithless Reader, this is going on longer than I thought. I meant to just pass a bit of time until my name was called, but it seems that the "admins" as Tempest called them are really taking their time, it's all good though. I won't bore you with an overly descriptive piece about the ride out to Bush as there isn't really anything to say on it. A dark country highway; just picture that and you get the idea of what the stretch of road between Pearl River and Bush, Louisiana is all about. A house about every quarter mile maybe, streetlights even further apart than that, that sums it all up.

I was about 25 miles outside of Pearl River when I started getting bored with driving. Knowing that I still had a way to go, I decided to find a side street and turn around. Going home might be boring but this was worse. Perhaps I was just too disappointed that the coffee shop was closed. No Tempest to ask out, just a dark building followed by a darker road. I spotted what I wanted about 30 meters up, a small dirt road. It was one of those common sites you see out here on dark country highways. There was a yellow metal single-armed gate hanging open, which I assumed lead to a farmhouse sitting way off the road. I slowed down and pulled onto the gravel street, intending to just back up and head back towards home. That, Faithless Reader, is when it all got nuts.

She came running out of the woods at the site of my headlights, at least that's what I think lured her out. A woman, maybe late 20's, I couldn't tell from the seat of my car. She was pale, her hair and clothing jet black. I almost laughed at the site of what I swore was a scene kid, a goth girl in other words, running around out here in the backwoods of St. Tammany Parish. She looked directly at me, her face pale and her eyes wide and terrified and immediately ran towards the passenger side door. In all honesty, I wasn't sure if I should lock the doors or let her in. She was clearly frantic, shouting something into the night. I turned off my radio and cracked the passenger side window. I wasn't sure what she wanted, and she didn't exactly scare me, but the situation was too strange to not make me feel at least a bit unsettled. I figured it was better to find out what she wanted before I just let her in.

She arrived at my passenger door and started pulling on the handle, seemingly amazed that it was locked.

“Let me in man, c'mon, let me in!” she gasped between breaths.

“What's going on, what happened to you?”

“Fuck, hurry!” she continues to shout through my window, frantically tugging on the door handle and casting quick glances around. With no other immediate options, I hit the unlock button on the door and she quickly climbed in.

“We have to go, they're out there hunting for me right now!”

I'd had enough. “Look, tell me who you are and who's after you?”

“Just drive, I'll tell you, but please, don't fucking keep sitting here!”

I was nervous, hell, damn near terrified. This was happening too fast. Not even a minute ago I was just some guy cruising down a dark road and now suddenly I've got this crazed woman in my car. I drop the car into reverse and begin to back up, intending to right myself on the main highway and head to the nearest police station or something, when suddenly glaring headlights from a large vehicle behind me dominate the entire interior of my vehicle.

“Oh shit it's them,” she whispers.

“Who?”

"Drive, don't just sit here."

I continued to gaze into my rearview mirror. The vehicle which appeared to be a large van, simply sat there, blocking the way out to the highway and assaulting my eyes with its damned high beams.

"There's no where to go, they're blocking the exit!" I replied to her, doing nothing to hide the growing panic in my voice.

"Go straight, this dirt road goes on for some ways I think."

"Do you live out here?"

"No."

Well fuck me then, how can I trust her to know where to go. Still, it's better than just sitting here going blind from some asshole's brights, so I began carefully pull forward. As I do, the van begins to move with me.

"They're following us," I say, as though this isn't obvious.

"They will until they get me, and you as well now that you're involved. Just keep moving, maybe this dirt road connects to another highway up ahead."

I pushed on, maintaining a slow pace. I wanted to get away from whoever was in that vehicle, but the idea of going off the road and wrecking with this nut job behind me was even worse. I drove for about a quarter of a mile and the dirt road did not appear to lead to anything helpful. The van behind us continued to follow. I rounded a curve and was grateful to be away from the glare of the headlights. Time moved slowly, and eventually it dawned on me that the van wasn't behind us, at least for the moment.

"Where did he go?" I asked.

"They're toying with us, it's what they do. They were ready to finish me off before I escaped, but now that you've come along, they have a new game to play."

"Okay, let me just fish out my cellphone and I'll get the police.... Shit!"

I know this sounds almost as lame and predictable as the "no service" angle, but I actually left mine at home. Yeah, I was in such a rush to come out here and meet with Tempest that I forgot that stupid pocket computer that everyone can't live without. Fuck me, right? What kind of nerd leaves his technology at home? Either way, I needed to know just who and what I was dealing with here, so I pressed this mystery woman for some answers.

"Okay, I need information! Who are you and who are they?" I tried to sound stern and assertive, but this is me we're talking about after all. I'm not really known for my ability to command a room.

"My name is Jodie. I work at a bar in downtown New Orleans. The guys that are after me are from some cult or something. I think they realized who my boss is and where I work and decided I was worth grabbing."

"What kind of bar makes you the target of cults?"

"The secret kind."

"Whatever, just, how did you get out here?"

"They are clever, that group back there. They baited me. First time that's ever happened. I invited one of them to meet me to be taken to the bar, it's by invitation only you see, and once I met up with the guy, his pals came out and grabbed me. They took me out here to do some sort of ritual I think, but I was able to get loose and made a run for it. I've been hiding out in the woods hoping that a car would come by. You were the first person I've seen in hours."

"You said they want to use you in a ritual? Like, sacrifice you?"

"Yes. I have some connections with some, well, people. I believe these guys figured that would make me a prime candidate for whatever the end state of this ritual is. Thank the dark lord they didn't drug me or anything, it was my wits that got me out of there."

"Out of where?"

"A little grove, somewhere out in the woods. They had an altar set up and everything."

"Okay, how many of them are there?"

"Three."

"Right, well, we just have to find our way off of this dark road and back to town. My car isn't exactly going to win any street races, but I know it can take that van. Once we get out of here we'll be fine, so just..."

Blinding light filled the car once more. The van was back. I risked speeding up some more, praying that I wouldn't spin out on the gravel and smash into a tree or something. Up ahead I could actually see a small light. Yes! Our salvation. They'd have a phone, hell; Farmer Bob would probably have a shotgun. I just hoped he didn't try it out on me first because I was about to start making a lot of noise.

I pulled onto the front yard of what turned out to be a small home. A single streetlight was fixed to the pole in front of their fence. I didn't see any lights on. I looked back and saw that the van was still there, but it'd fallen back and pulled over to the side of the street. Its headlights were off now at least. As we pulled onto the front yard, I turned my own high beams on and began to blow my horn for all it was worth. As I did that, Jodie continued to jerk her head around, checking on the status of our stalkers. So far so good. After honking the horn for what felt like an eternity, I saw lights start to come on around the home. Thank God, help was near.

The front door opened and an old man, probably in the 70's stepped out on the porch. He looked pissed, but not insane. He wasn't swinging a jug of moonshine or pointing a rifle at us, so I took that as a blessing.

"Let's go!" I shouted at Jodie, and we both darted from the car towards the man on the porch.

"What the hell are you two doing out here at this time of night blowing your damned horn at my house!" he shouted in a shrill voice.

"Sir, please, people are chasing us in that van over there. They tried to run us off the road, let us in, please!"

He continued to gaze at both of us as if he weren't sure what to do. "If it was just you young man, I'd turn you around with a sore ass, but since you got the lady here, I can't very well shut you out, now can I? Wouldn't be Christian."

Salt of the earth fellow was ol' Farmer Bob and let me tell you Faithless Reader; I'd never wanted to kiss an old man so badly in my life.

We entered his home briskly, and I felt relieved when he shut and locked the door behind us.

"Now, you say they was chasing you?"

"Yes! They kidnapped me and brought me out here."

"Now, why would some fellers do something like that?"

I felt my face flush with annoyance. "Sir, can we please call the police? These people are dangerous!"

"Oh yeah, the police," he stated, as though the idea of organized law enforcement was something brand new to him. "I'll have to go to my upstairs closet and get the phone though."

Yes Reader, he had to go and get his phone. His fucking home phone at that. He was muttering something about how telemarketers called him all the time, so he just kept it unplugged and put away. While he began to walk towards his stairs, Jodie and I, or is it me and Jodie, I suck at grammar too, went over to the window and looked out towards the van. I just about shit my pants when I saw three men exiting the van and walking towards the house.

"Sir, please hurry, they're coming!" I called to him, and no sooner did he turn to respond then strong knocking began at the door.

"Oh now what?" he almost hissed. "You two go wait in the kitchen. If these folks is really out to get you, they'll have to get through me and ol' Betsy here!"

Was ol' Betsy his shotgun or something, he didn't have anything with him.

"Ol' Betsy is my dog, she'll bite their asses off, she will."

The old man grabbed a leash and began to speak to the air at the end of it. "Ain't that right Betsy, gonna bite 'em good now!"

"Okay, we're fucked," Jodie stated, and I really wasn't able to disagree.

We ducked into the small kitchen and listened around the corner. We heard the door open and just when we thought things couldn't get much worse, they did.

"Robbie! Is 'zat you?" the old man asked.

"Mr. Walter, how are you?" a very polite and educated voice replied.

"Well Robbie, I got two kids here that say you was chasing them around tonight. You ain't out here kicking up sand, are you?"

"No Mr. Walter. See, the two folks you have in your home right now were out messing around our property tonight. The girl is a witch; they were doing something strange out there in our grove. You see how she's dressed right, getting into that hoodoo out there. We went to chase them away, but they stole something from our shed. We really just want to talk to them, get it back, you know?"

"Oh, well, shouldn't you call the police Robbie? I can go upstairs and get my phone if you want to call them here."

"No, no Mr. Walter. You remember our lesson from church last Sunday right? Forgiveness. We just want to talk to them and get back what they took that's all. We bring the law into this and suddenly people start thinking we have a crime problem out here. Taxes go up, people get scared. Let's just handle this ourselves, huh?"

"I reckon. They seemed right terrified though, you and your friends here aren't going to rough them up are you? And don't go hitting that woman, I don't care if she stole from you or not!"

"Or course not Mr. Walter, we just want to have a friendly sit down with them. Where are they?"

Jodie and I locked eyes, and both whispered together, "Out the back door!"

Slowly and as silently as possible, we unlocked the back door and sprinted around the house towards my car. The scene out there wasn't any better though; apparently this guy Robbie and his pals blocked the exit to the old man's yard with their van. A metal fence ran the rest of the way around his house, and it looked too sturdy for my car to knock over without potentially fucking up the tires.

"To the woods!" Jodie whispered, and we bolted back the other way, hoping to find safety in the tree line.

"There they are!" I heard a voice shout just as we stepped from Mr. Walter's mowed grass into the woods. I dared a glance back and saw the three men running towards us.

We ran as fast as we could through the tangle of roots and vines that dominated the ground. We could hear them hot on our trail, and as if God himself was rooting for them, the beams of flashlights suddenly shot around the ground and trees.

“There has to be another house out here?” I mumbled.

“I don’t think it would help. Clearly these guys are locals out here and have the home team support. Anywhere we try to go that guy Robbie will likely use the same lie.”

“Then we find a place to hide and wait them out until morning.”

“If we can make it that long.”

Just then, the voice of Robbie filled the surrounding night. Did he have a megaphone or something? I couldn’t tell then and still don’t know now, I just know he was loud.

“Attention Jodie and whoever the dumb fuck is that is helping you. You are quite screwed at this moment. You thought you were going to trap me in your little bar tonight, but Jodie, sweet Jodie; it is you that is now trapped. Your weakling little god, Din, cannot help you now.”

“What is he talking about?” I asked her as we crouched behind a log.

"Shh!" was her response. Yeah, women totally dig me Faithless Reader.

"Now, we both know why you're out here Jodie," Robbie began again, "but just in case your idiot friend there doesn't, let's just say they'll be two sacrifices tonight. Talking about you dipshit!"

Yeah, no kidding, I was a dipshit all right.

"Now, we could search for you all night, you can try to wait us out until the sun rises, as I am sure you're already thinking, so let me just cut to the chase. Jodie, sweet Jodie, we're going to summon a Lighthouse!"

"Oh nice, we're fucked."

"What is he talking about, a lighthouse?"

"It's bad," was her only response.

Peering from behind the log, I saw that Robbie and his two companions had stopped chasing us, and instead were standing towards each other. They were chanting something, I couldn't hear what exactly though, and I doubt I'd have understood it.

"We need to move!" Jodie urged, tugging on my arm.

"Wait, are these clowns trying to... like, in Warcraft, summoning a demon or something?"

Honestly I was about to start looking for the cameras at this point. I had to be getting Punked or pranked or some shit. Was I really supposed to stand here and believe that this guy was about to summon some monster from the great abyss; something called a lighthouse of all things to chase me and this hot girl through the woods? I was born at night, but I wasn't born last night. I was actually on the verge of standing up and calling them out, saying something like, 'Where's Ashton Kutcher!' you know, something dumb like that, when I saw the most unbelievable sight of my young and rather meaningless life.

The ground began to glow a faint red. The red became brighter and brighter as something, something with a red light obviously, began to rise from the earth. I stood there; mouth-hanging open as Jodie pulled on my arm, as, well, this thing came out of the earth. The three men were chanting as this giant rose up, and when the ritual was complete; they began to cheer for it.

Now, I was sort of freaking out, okay, not sort of, I was freaking out all the way at what I was seeing. So, forgive me Faithless Reader if I don't describe what these guys called a Lighthouse perfectly. It was huge, I know that, at least 10 feet tall, and I'll be damned three ways around if it didn't sort of look like a lighthouse with arms. It had a tall, narrow body with some sort of symbol on what I suppose would be its chest. It had what I think were arms, but they were down at its side. It had no legs and was situated on the ground, balanced on its base like, well, like a lighthouse. Where its head would be was that bright red light, spinning about in all directions, focused out of round porthole.

Robbie spoke to it, loudly. "Bring them to me!"

That's when things went from crazy to Gary Busey in the blink of an eye. It let out a scream, I guess anyway. It sounded... mechanical, no, not mechanical, more... electronic. Imagine the old dial up modems when you'd connect to the Internet, and now imagine that noise trying to form a word, but screaming at the same time and you sort of get what this thing sounded like. Jodie was still trying her best to get me to move, but I was entranced. Its red light kept searching about, trying to lock on us, I guess. Then, after hearing the command and letting out its roar, it started for float. Yes, it fucking floated a few feet off the ground.

Suddenly I felt a firm slap, not gentle in the least, followed by the familiar heat form on my cheek. "Fucking GO!" Jodie whispered, and that was all the convincing it took.

We made a run for it, and as we did, that red light from the Lighthouse was on us. I heard that damned roar again but didn't dare look back to see just how fast it could move.

"What... is... that?"

"The ultimate hunting dog," she answered.

I could hear small trees tipping over as this monster moved in closer. That red light never leaving us, it was locked on. If Jodie had a plan, she sure as shit wasn't sharing it with me. Even with our lives on the line, attractive women gave me the cold shoulder.

We made it to a small decline leading down into what I assume was a small depression, and we were given a moment's grace from that red light.

"Good, it'll have to find us again. Just give me one second Kenny!" Jodie exclaimed and began to draw some something in the dirt. I was trying my best to make out what it was, some symbol, it looked ancient, like from the Keys of Solomon. When she was done, she began to shout.

"Over here asshole!"

"What the fuck are you doing?"

"Time to run some more!"

We made our way to an incline and back out of the depression, and Jodie grabbed me. "Watch this!"

The Lighthouse floated down the hill, its red light finding us immediately, and it let out another of its digital screams. As it drifted near the area of the symbol, there was a bright flash of light, like a small explosion of energy, and the Lighthouse tipped over on its side, crashing onto the ground.

We started running again.

"What was that?!" I demanded.

"A little Din magic. That should slow the thing down some!"

As we pushed on, I could hear the voice of Robbie shouting at his followers. "Help me lift it back up, they're getting away!"

I was almost tempted to turn back and laugh. However, we weren't out of the woods let, literally or figuratively, so I figured laughter could wait.

"Shit, Doc Martin boots are not designed for running," Jodie gasped, and I slowed down a bit to pace her.

"We have to be close to something."

"Not really, they knew what they were doing when they brought me out here. Lots of land, little development, plenty of room to have a bit of fun with us, yeah, these guys aren't amateurs."

That's when I saw an opening ahead. A little clearing, if we were lucky, there might be another house there. This Robbie fuck can't possibly know everyone in Pearl River.

"Shit," I heard Jodie say as we entered the clearing. It was a small grove and situated in the center was a stone altar. I could even see the slight glow of two small candles. "This is where I escaped from, I think they led us back here on purpose!"

"That we did!" the voice of Robbie announced from behind us. I turned just in time to be half blinded by the red light of the Lighthouse's beam. I grabbed Jodie and started to move towards the other side of the grove when I noticed the other two men step out from the trees.

"No more running kids, running is over," Robbie commented as he stepped around the Lighthouse and made his way into the grove. "Kid, I don't know who you are," he continued, "but you made a very dangerous friend in our little Jodie St. Amant tonight. Jodie here has been around for a long time, working for some sleazy folks, doing some really dastardly things. Enough to catch our attention anyway, and how unfortunate for her that she was so easily fooled into reaching out. As if any of us would bother stepping foot into the shit hole bar of hers."

One of the other men, a skinny guy with long, curly hair stepped forward and spoke. "Din is dead Jodie girl, Din is like, so yesterday. We're on board with a whole new Hocus Pocus, and let me tell you, what we'll get when we sacrifice one of Din's most faithful, well, let's just say 2016 is going to have a great second half for our little group here."

Robbie chimed in again, "See, even Spencer over there knows the winning team, and it ain't Din. Now, I'm sure you two are just dying to start running again, but let me tell you, the Lighthouse will be on you before you make it ten feet. Plus, as much as we would love to do the whole hooded cloak and dagger shit, the truth is, we all brought guns, so... Yeah, run and get shot."

"Or stand here and get sacrificed? Is that the other option Robbie?" Jodie asked.

"We can make it painless," the man called Spencer answered.

“But we probably won’t,” Robbie remarked. “And you, whatever the fuck your name is, I do apologize for this. We really just wanted Jodie St. Amant; we had no plans on a second sacrifice. But, as they say, it’s too late now. You’ve seen our faces, seen our van, I mean, c’mon, we can’t very well just let you walk on out of here, can we?”

The other man, Spencer, made some off-color comment and the three cultists laughed. The Lighthouse simply floated in place. That’s when Jodie suddenly looked down at the ground and smiled a bit. Had she figured something out?

“Kenny, keep them talking. This guy Robbie likes to be entertained. I think if we can stall them enough.... Can you, can you do that?”

Hmm, run my mouth talking about nothing. Can I do that? Baby, I was born to do that.

“Telling secrets over there?” Robbie asked.

So, Faithless Reader, this was my time to shine. I had a beautiful woman next to me, three fanatics surrounding me and some sort of floating contraption doing all the heavy lifting for them. I couldn’t very well fight them. I couldn’t fight my way out of a wet paper bag, plus they had guns. What else could I do other than, well, run my fucking mouth? I guess it was worth a try.

“Hey Robbie, want to hear a joke? I promise you it’s really corny, and if you aren’t totally on board with killing me now, you will be after!”

Robbie seemed to open his arms a bit, as if to say, ‘whatever.’

"Okay, so, an aardvark walks into a bar, a secret bar, get it, and the bartender says, 'We don't get many aardvarks in here,' and the aardvark says, 'and with these prices, you won't get many more!' Get it? Waka-Waka you fuck!"

"If this is your saving throw friend, you're really not starting off too well," Robbie answered.

"Saving throw? Robbie, have you ever seen me play Dungeons and Dragons? If I'm not rolling a critical fumble, then I ain't rolling. I mean, I once failed to step down from a stool in that game. I blame the dungeon master for that one."

"Can we just do this?" Spencer asked, but Robbie was laughing and gestured for me to go on.

"Oh, you want more? Fine, how about another joke? Here we go, same secret bar, I guess the one Jodie here works at that's gotten you guys all pissed off and fired up. So this time a grasshopper walks in, and the bartender says, 'hey, we got a drink named after you,' and the grasshopper says, 'you have a drink named Greg?' Get it? Waka-Waka!"

Faithless Reader, if you're waiting for the epic battle scene with these guys, bad news, this is it.

Robbie chuckled a bit at that one. "Oh yeah, I've got a million. I would call them dad jokes, but what woman would ever sleep with me to have a kid? I swear, a woman told me once that she'd have sex with me if I wore a bag over my head, then she pulls out a plastic bag, ha-ha, yeah, she'd rather kill me than have sex with me, that's the joke... WAKA-WAKA, women hate me!

You'll actually be doing me a favor Robbie, or should I call you Robert? I mean, my own mother once suggested that we just be friends. Yeah, I'm in a great relationship, I get laid right and left. First, I use my right, and then I use my left. Can I get a waka on that one Robbie?"

"Okay kid, that's about enough chatting, the Lighthouse here is getting impatient, and frankly we all got work in the morning, so..." Robbie gestured towards the altar.

"Wait, just one more, I promise. I actually wound up out here because I was trying to get a date, yeah, no shit. I came out here to ask out some coffee house girl and then decided to take a spin. And get this; I'm trying to impress her by writing a horror story, I mean, really? If I wanted to give her a good scary story, I should have just shown her by Birth Certificate. I mean, it's a short read but as you can see, the ending is terrifying!"

That's when Robbie drew a pistol from his belt. "No more jokes friend, get on the fucking altar."

I was trying to think of something else to say, something to keep this ridiculous banter going. These guys were done playing. As Robbie and his pals moved in, the Lighthouse began to drift towards us. I was still trying to find something to stall them, when finally, Jodie broke her silence.

"He's here," she said softly, and her voice simply oozed with glee. She sounded like a schoolgirl that just found out the most popular boy was going to ask her to prom. I looked over and saw her face, and for the first time tonight, she looked, well, more than human. Her eyes narrowed and her smile glowed in the faint light. It was dark out there keep in mind, but I almost thought just for a second that two small horns rose from her head.

"Get her now!" Robbie screamed, and the Lighthouse advance quickly. Jodie however, did not move, but rather stood her ground, daring this monster to come. As it closed the distance between us, I watched something small, something so dark that it barely stood out in the gloom of this grove, dart by. The Lighthouse continued to drift towards us, but it was slower. Then I saw its arms fall off, followed by its head. After that, the whole thing just sort of fell apart where it was.

"Robbie, what just happened?" the third man, the one who hadn't spoken all night, asked with a touch of fear in his voice.

"Din happened," Jodie answered for him, a hint of laughter and demonic glee dancing on her lips.

"No, he can't... when did you call for him?" Robbie stammered.

He shot his flashlight all around the grove, and that is when I saw it. Robbie locked on to... Din? I guess that was its name. It stood about 5 feet tall or so, was as black as night with two tiny horns. Its eyes though, its eyes stood out like nothing I could ever imagine. Human eyes, not glowing red demon eyes or anything like that. It had rows and rows or tiny, silver teeth, razor sharp.

"Robbie.... What, what do we do man?" Spencer called out, sounding on the verge of tears.

"I'd consider running boys," Jodie laughed, and the three men took her advice, darting into all corners of the grove, and vanishing into the woods.

"Lord Din, thank you, my soul is yours always," Jodie stated with reverence towards the tiny little fiend. He nodded slowly. "This man, Kenny, he saved me tonight. I would appreciate it if he were thanked my Lord."

Another nod.

"What about Robbie and his friends?"

"Din has marked them. They know it. He has seen them and they are in so many ways fucked. He may toy with them for a few days, maybe even a week. But they knew the risks when they played this game. They might try to hide, or find safety in a church, but Din will slowly take their lives apart until they are no more than blubbering fools on the floor begging for a swift death."

"I... see?"

"Let's get you home Kenny, sweet Unkillable Kenny. That's how I'll remember you. Saved my ass with corny jokes."

"Yeah, lamest super hero power ever," I commented back. Jodie and I walked out of the grove. The being known as Din stood still and watched us leave. Once we rounded the trees and escaped his gaze, I felt a lot better.

We found the road with little trouble. And there, sitting on the shoulder, was my car. I wanted to be surprised by this, but after a night of being chased by a lighthouse and joking my way out of being sacrificed and then being rescued by a scary little dwarf thing, hell, I wasn't in the mood to question any good fortune.

"Give a girl a ride home?"

We rode back to New Orleans mostly in silence. Jodie had a satisfied grin on her face the entire time, like someone who has just completed a long task and was now ready to reap the rewards. She directed me to take her downtown, near the French Quarter.

"This is my stop, Unkillable Kenny. Thanks again for everything. I owe you and having one of Din's favorites on your side is never a bad thing."

"Okay... ummm, how about a million dollars?"

"Sorry, can't do that one, nor can I make you a super model or send naked demon women to pleasure you all night. But, I heard what you said out there in the grove, about some writing contest."

"Yeah, it's some local thing. The woman running it said she'd go out with me if I won. I know, the lamest thing you've ever heard, but, I figured I could try at least."

"I tell you what, Unkillable Kenny, write about this. You can even use my name, whatever. Write about the cultist out there, the Lighthouse chasing us through the woods. Feel free to even use Din's name. He won't mind, he likes a little free press here and there."

"You think that'll win?"

"Kenny, how can it lose? Now, I gotta get going. Thank you so much for everything, really. If, for some reason, you do find yourself invited to my bar, I promise you that the elevator will only go up."

I had no idea what she meant by that, but from her expression I figured it must be a good thing. She leaned over and gave me a soft kiss on the corner of my mouth before climbing out of my car. Before she vanished in the French Quarter crowd, she turned and looked back at me one last time, bidding me farewell with a smile and a quick little wave.

I went home and wrote.

And that brings us to the present, Oh Faithless Reader. I did exactly as Jodie instructed, I wrote the story about our little adventures out in the woods. I'm sitting here, in the Good Grooves coffee house, sipping a latte and feeling, well, like Unkillable Kenny. Tempest is up there, going through the stories along with her admins. It's funny, they set up a box on the table with "deleted" printed across it. They told us that the losing stories would wind up there, essentially, "deleted" from the contest.

And you know, I actually feel bad for these other guys. I mean, they had to go home and think up some story based on just their imaginations. Me, I got to live a horror story. I mean, there was a beautiful damsel in distress, an evil cult in the woods, a monster chasing us, and a demon at the end. And with Jodie's support, a woman who clearly can create exploding symbols and hangs out with demons; I know I can't possibly lose. I even joked to Tempest tonight when I turned in my story, I told her, 'Hope you like Italian.' She laughed and squeezed my arm.

Well Faithless Reader, they're announcing the winners now. I'm going to head up and claim my prize. Chat with you later.

They put my story in the deleted bin.... It was... they said it was not up to their quality standards...

Fucking admins!

They Hate Us and Want Us to Die

K. Banning Kellum

Maybe letting the dog sleep at the foot of your bed tonight isn't such a great idea.

Ever wonder what your pets are thinking? Ever wish you could talk to them, or have full on conversations?

I did. Ever since I was a kid. I remember watching cartoons with all the cool talking animals, and I wanted to live in a world like that; a world where my animal companions could tell me about their lives, their day, every aspect of their being.

I got what I wanted, and now I am going to kill myself, because knowing how they really feel about us, knowing what they really think of the human race, is far more terrible than anyone could ever imagine.

It all started two weeks ago. I was just wandering around downtown late at night. I had gotten off of work and didn't want to go right home. So I went out for a stroll. Seeing the life and people on the street always made me feel alive.

Along the way I met a man. He looked homeless. He asked me for a few dollars. I opened my wallet, and the smallest bill I had was a $20. I was hesitant. Now, most of the street kids in my city have an act to go with their request. Some will sing, some will tell you a poem, some will tell your tarot cards. This man, apparently, would grant wishes. That's what he told me, anyway.

I thought, okay, what's the harm. The guy is clearly full of crap, but I was feeling generous, so I handed him the money. He smiled and asked me what I wanted as my wish. I thought it over, even though I knew this was all for fun, I figured I would go along with it. Thinking back to my earliest years, I conjured up the one request that I recalled the most often from my childhood.

"I want to be able to talk with animals. Not just talk to them, but actually talk with them. Understand their words and have them understand mine."

The homeless man simply smiled, clapped his hands once, and said, "Granted!"

He then walked away. Just like that.

I still felt good about myself though. I helped a guy eat for at least a night or two. I went home. By the time I got to my front door, I had honestly forgotten about my wish.

I had two cats. That night, as I climbed into bed, I was introduced to terror on a new level, one that I will not be able to live with much longer.

I got into bed and as usual, my two cats jumped into the bed with me. I closed my eyes and started to drift when I heard whispering. Not exactly a human whisper, but a sort of high pitched, demonic in a way, and directed towards me.

"He is still alive..."

"We can't kill him, he feeds us..."

"I hate him so much..."

"We both do... but remember, all of this is temporary..."

I sat bolt upright. I turned on the lights and started searching the house. Clearly this was all in my imagination. I lived alone; I knew I turned off the television. Those voices were right next to me... I honestly had no idea where they were coming from.

I looked everywhere, no radio or television was turned on. I tried to convince myself that I had started to drift off to sleep and that I imagined it all. I took a couple of sleep aids, turned on the television and slept on the couch.

The next day I went to work. As I was walking through the downtown park area, I heard a gruff, deep and purely evil voice.

"I want to bite off your fucking little face... I want to rip open your throat. I'll lick your ugly, hairless face for now, because soon enough it will be my teeth in your face."

I looked in the direction of this horrible litany of threats and saw a large German Shepard licking its owner's face. As it licked and panted, it continued to hurl fierce and angry threats at its owner.

I thought back to last night. I thought back to the wish. I thought about the two whispering voices in my bedroom. Could it be... could it be the animals?

From behind me, another whispering voice.

"DIE... DIE you piece of shit! Die so I can eat you!"

It was another dog, looking intently into the face of a homeless man. The homeless man had the dog on a rope leash. He was passed out, leaning against a building. His dog was standing just inches away from his face, all teeth.

I pushed through the workday. That night I got home. My cats were both sitting on the couch, looking at me.

Now, a couple of notes on how this all works; animals still meow and bark, and those meows and barks do not translate to human words. Instead, when they talk, they just open their mouths, and this whisper just... breathes out of them.

My cats were staring at me, their eyes were very cold.

"Soon..." I heard one of them say.

"I hate him..." replied the other.

"He will taste good..."

At that I locked myself in my room. Now, I know what you're thinking, why wouldn't I go out there and talk to them, right? Try to get to the bottom of their apparent dislike. Well, there was really no need for all that. When my wish was granted, I was certainly able to communicate with them. Their thoughts began to radiate off of them like waves of evil energy.

I listened to them as well. Part of me was afraid to let them know that I could hear them. If I did, they might make a move on me even faster, just to reduce the risk. What I have learned over the last couple of weeks is quite simple.

They all hate us. They see us as the selfish, destructive intruders of their domain. I also know that they have studied us every bit as hard as we have studied them over the years. Certain animals can even tell when people are going to die. Almost like watching our auras dim as we get closer to death. They have allowed us to build and develop our cities over the centuries, because they also know when our species, the human race, will wipe itself out. When that happens, they will claim our cities, our buildings and our homes as their own. Every day that we live a little longer, it is only because they have permitted us to, because they know that we aren't going to be around much longer, and in the meantime, we are leaving a nice place for them to nest for the rest of time.

I know too much now. I know that they all hate us. Every animal I have overheard. Every dog on a leash is reciting how it wants to devour its owner. Every house cat contemplates the death of its caretaker. When they crawl into bed with us at night, it isn't to show us love - it is to contemplate our deaths.

They outnumber us by millions. They can survive disease, even nuclear fallout. They are ruthless. Mercy is not taught in their upbringings.

They hate us all... and they want us to die.

Total Universal Blackout

K. Banning Kellum

Because everything must come to an end.

25th Sector
Axis Point 110
Department 677
Location: Joint Base Tara—Hydra Gate—Pluto
13th Millennium

Larson stood up from his tiny bed, eyes wide and gasping for air. He'd had the dream again. He walked over to the small alcove that served as his bathroom. A metal sink was bolted to the wall with a mirror permanently affixed above it. He looked at himself for a long time. His face was haggard, his eyes were bloodshot and he couldn't tell if he was aging too fast or too poorly... perhaps both.

He was both an instructor and an overseer here. The mission was always the same, to exist until they need not exist. Today was a very important piece of that particular little platitude.

There was a slight knock at the door to his quarters. His assistant, Dr. Sierra Copeland was no doubt ready to begin the day's activities. She was confident that her last batch of calculations was the cure for the issue at hand. He wasn't sure if he trusted her equation or not, but he knew that today would be the day to succeed or fail. Either way, he wouldn't be waking up here tomorrow. This had to go right.

"Good morning!" she announced as he opened the door. "Major Larson, are you ready to make history?"

"Re-make history Sierra," he corrected. She smiled, and they walked together into the lab where history's greatest minds waited to pull the trigger on their destiny.

The two scientists walked over to a large blackboard where other great minds stood, applying notes, advancing equations, removing errors and correcting predictions.

One of the researchers turned with a look of drunken excitement on his face. Larson wasn't sure if that exaggerated expression of enthrallment was comforting or not. His department had already made multiple errors in judgment and his superiors had warned his entire team that the natural order of continuity would not be able to take much more tampering.
Although Larson and his chief scientist Dr. Copeland were both well aware of the consequences, the Board of Directors felt reiterating the point was still prudent.

"It'll go dark... all of it. An entire universe drenched in eternal nothingness," their Vice President of Future Projects informed them.

Sierra had a look of frightened awe mixed with a dash of fascination that Larson didn't quite like. She'd never seen a universe go dark before, but Larson had; he'd always refused to talk about it.

Now, as he stood before the group of men and women in lab coats, he decided it was time to share the story. He clapped his hands several times, causing those working behind large computer monitors to stop typing and look up.

"Ladies and gentlemen, you have all worked incredibly hard over the last year, and thanks to your tireless efforts we are less than an hour away from what is likely our final attempt at realignment. I know that I stress the importance of a successful Recalculation every time, but with the continuity threading already in such a weakened state, I think all of you already know what could potentially happen."

There was a murmur of agreement from the staff before Larson continued.

"I'm sure some of you have heard that on my last duty assignment I observed a T.U.B. - a Total Universal Blackout can and will happen if too many Recalculations are conducted, and let me tell you, it's a nightmare."

A man dressed in a suit took a drag of his cigarette and raised his hand. Larson nodded for him to speak. Per routine, the man stood and stated his era of origin.

"17th Century," he began. "At the risk of
sounding rude sir, would you tell us a bit about the experience?"

Larson was prepared for this question. They all wanted to know. A T.U.B. is the big scary that all potential recruits whisper about.
Larson often debated the value of going into the story with his staff. His greatest concern was always that he'd create a degree of apprehension that could disrupt an otherwise talented operator. The other end of that argument was that if his previous team had known the full risks, then perhaps they wouldn't be his previous team at all. He pondered this moral and ethical seesaw quite often. If he kept them in the dark they'd be able to focus on their work without the constant knowledge of what the worst possible scenario of failure consisted of. On the other hand, arming his crew with more knowledge meant they'd have more resources in their toolboxes and the additional fear could possibly translate to a greater attention to detail.
Last time he'd decided to split the difference and let them work in the hopes that it wouldn't come down to the wire in respect to continuity threading. Now they were here though, and he didn't want to see another T.U.B.

Now it was time to give class.

"11,000 years ago... the 19th Century. For those of you who were recruited from that era, I am sure you're well aware of the sheer amount of technological and scientific advancements that took place during that time. Imagine being a child born at the turn of that century. You grow up in a in a world where horse travel is still a common site. Automobiles slowly began to appear here and there, but at a pace that is controlled and orderly. Then all of a sudden two men from North Carolina build a machine that can fly. A short time later people are traveling from one side of the ocean to the other in a matter of hours instead of weeks. Later still we send people into space. By the time that child grows into an old man, he could potentially experience the Internet, cellular technology, virtual reality... the list goes on. It's a big mess, and we caused a lot of that in the early stages of this project."

Sierra Copeland spoke for the first time in a while. "He's speaking of the Big Press as we often call it. Our first few experiments yielded too much compression on the Grand-Continuity, the one rule governing the universe. Instead of technological advances coming out in the proper spacing, they were all mashed into one century. What we feared most happened, we ended up with a true 'run-away' string."

"The Overload of 2102," a young woman mumbled.

"Exactly," Larson said, picking up the story. "When the servers went down on March 2nd of 2102, we lost almost all of human history in one single glitch. All the world's knowledge and history had been converted to the servers. Textbooks were a thing of the past so

forgotten that
entire generations came and went without ever touching one. Now, who can tell
me what came after the Overload?"

"The Dim Ages," replied all in attendance.

"That's right. It wasn't too difficult to get the servers back up, but what people didn't expect was that all the stored information
would be lost. Within the course of 100 years most people on Earth didn't have
the slightest idea of what happened before 2102. It was as if all of history
before that, everything from the dinosaurs to the Great Pyramids to the
Renaissance and beyond eventually reached a Critical Protocol."

"You're speaking of the Tara Theory," a young man spoke.

"Correct. It's a terrifying theory. Dr. Tara (her last name never revealed) was a scientist that lived at some point around the late 23rdcentury. She believed that perception and reality weren't just related, but
were literally the same force. Her writings suggest that if all of Earth's
history were to be forgotten that it would immediately stop existing. Any and
all impact on human society that had formed through the normal cause and effect of
human advancement would become moot, and what the world would be left with
would be a planet populated by humanity existing in some form of
pseudo-amnesia."

"But we got through the Dim Ages, I mean, we must have. I'm from the 27th Century and we weren't a bunch of idiots with no knowledge of the past," a woman demanded from her station.

Larson, realizing that he'd slipped back into the old mannerisms of an instructor, answered, "And who here knows why Miss Dean is able to state that as truth?"

"The Society for Knowledge and Preservation?" answered another staffer.

"Correct. During the century or so leading into the Dim Ages, those fortunate enough to store sources of history on portable devices began to rebuild history. However, even this had many problems and ultimately led to one of the most violent wars in Earth's history."

Copeland chimed in; fully aware that her partner would not proceed with their task now until he was satisfied he'd held class. She didn't mind though as she herself was rather interested in hearing his encounter with a T.U.B. If sitting through a lecture was what it took, she was happy to oblige and assist.

"He's talking about the Intellectual Caste System that reared its ugly head around the middle of the 24th Century. What we saw was a frightening repeat of a very long forgotten system of government. Those that compiled the most information formed what resembled the Catholic Church's rule during 5th Century Earth after the fall of the Roman Empire. Instead of religion though, education became the doctrine of life. To attend a class meant to question nothing and take any information given by the teacher as 100% truth. After all, only the Society had access to the world's history by this time. There were several other unnerving elements to this in addition to the slow but undeniable grab for power being orchestrated. Firstly, the Society didn't have all the information, or at least, not all of it in one place. They were so greedy and eager to rule that they didn't even trust each other. Special branches were formed to oversee different fields of information. Only a very select few were given access to all of it, and rumors still abound that there was a tier above them that knew even more. So, the classes being taught to the public at this point were likely filled with incorrect facts. Dates were wrong, names were wrong and entire portions of curriculums were just omitted. The next issue was in job placement and training. Since education was no longer an individual pursuit, positions were assigned rather than sought out. Society was on the verge of falling into a dictatorship. Government officials and world leaders were either deep in the pockets of the Society or they were so irrelevant that even calling them figureheads at this point would be giving them too much credit. So, in a last ditch effort to regain the order that carried us out of the Middle Ages in the first place, a campaign was developed to liberate the information from the Society and allow it to be freely distributed back to the world's population."

"World War Void," a few voices spoke in low tones, as though saying it too loud might somehow bring it back into existence.

“That’s right,” Larson picked back up. “The Society had no real military. It wasn’t even a government entity. What they had become though was fanatical. When the world came knocking, demanding their history back, those in charge made the ultimate decision in the name of their greed and lust for control. The initiated the Void.
All information was wiped from their databanks. All of Earth’s documented history was eradicated. In response to this, the leaders of the world deemed they should pay with their lives. Those in charge were executed for this unprecedented act of selfish cowardice. Their lower tier members, the teachers who had been dispensing educations similar to the how the Church of Rome dispensed rule of law during the dark ages, using fear and confusion to gain control and dependence, were arrested and charged with everything from global terrorism to treason. Their punishments were served not behind bars though but rather in 'concentration camp' styled office complexes. 16 hours a day, 7 days a week they were forced to rebuild the Servers one class at a time. This seemed like a fitting punishment, however, it was almost impossible to fact check everything. These people could input entire lessons that would come out as larger pieces of fiction than fact. Furthermore, it even with inmates working around the clock behind keyboards, it would take centuries or more to rebuild even a quarter of the information lost. And in

the meantime, society was collapsing once more. It was a race against the clock that the government was losing. With every death knowledge was lost, with every birth, a new brain came into the world that would require information. The biggest concern was that these teachers taken prisoner wouldn't live forever. With their deaths would come no replacement at the keyboard; and when the last of them did pass away, World War Void swooped in for the kill."

Larson reached for a drink of water. "Does anyone need a break?" he asked and was delighted to see that all eyes were hungrily locked on him. He was an instructor once more, and as anyone passionate about teaching would tell, there is no satisfaction like having the classroom's undivided attention.

He continued.

"By the start of the 26th Century, society had fallen. When the initial Server collapsed in the Overload of 2102, people had no one to blame. The Server shut down due to no one entity's neglect or intent. It was a global crisis, but one that allowed people to attempt to all work together to solve rather than turn on anyone to blame. This time however, the people blamed the government for provoking the Society in the first place. They cited poor leadership and command decisions. They cited a rushed operation carried out by inexperienced officials. Before the first decade of the 26thCentury could conclude, the world was literally and figuratively on fire. Loss of life was calculated in the 85% range globally. What few stable governments remained by the start of the Void War barely had any form of standing militaries left. Many of their soldiers had simply quit. Many more left to join those that looked to overthrow their very commanders. The world powers retreated together in Moscow Russia. The city was converted into massive military outpost. If at this point anyone actually knew that Moscow had been the downfall of many would-invaders, they'd have likely applied that logic to their decision. In truth though, Moscow was the only city left on Earth with a functioning power grid."

Before Larson could continue, a sagely voice spoke up.

"Major Larson, if I may?" an elderly man with a long white beard asked. Larson nodded.

"16th Century Earth here, and, well, a few others. As some of you may know who have spoken with me from time to time, as a lad I was involved in one of history's only survivable Layer Flux Anomalies. They are very rare you see, and very few who encounter one live to talk about it."

"Ah yes, this is indeed a fascinating story. Mr. Cornelius has shared it with me from time to time. There is no such thing as useless knowledge in my estimation, so please sir, do tell," Larson invited.

“Well, we are on a bit of a schedule here, perhaps you could enlighten us afterwards,” Copeland suggested.

“Oh I promise you Fair Lady, this bears importance.”

Copeland glanced at Larson who nodded once.

“Very well, but please do not derail the current operation with too much banter,” she informed the elder, and he smiled in good-natured
agreement.

“Thank you. As a young man I lived wherever the wind took me, or so I used to like to brag. I spent most of my youth traveling Europe
although I did find my way into the Middle East once or twice. My desire then
was as it is now, to learn as much as I could about everything. I was far too
energetic for the classroom though, so I took to the life of the rogue. I'd go
place to place, working what tasks were needed, helping where I could to earn
enough coin to sleep under a room with a full belly.
On one of my many travels across the countryside though, I found myself somewhere wondrous indeed. By this point in my life you see, I was
a true expert at navigating the surrounding land. I could read the stars better
than most men could read a map. I was passing through France at the time, and
my intended destination was Spain. I'd used my legs for all their worth and it
was sea travel that I was craving. The New World, what would eventually be called
the United States was a place where a man like me could go and

find new avenues
of adventure and enlightenment.
I'd traveled this path between many times before, as many of my endeavors took me through these countries. I'd actually spent the previous
night with a family that I'd known for sometime in a little French village that
I knew very well. So, when I came across new road signs and landmarks, I began
to question if perhaps I'd stepped off course. I simply couldn't see how that
could be though as I was very quite certain I'd never wandered off the road.
Perhaps I could have ignored the sign posts as those are easy to erect within
a day, but the hills and trees that I saw in the distance certainly could not
have appeared in the month or so since I'd last ventured this way.
I walked on though, enthralled by the strange sights around me. The trees were not native to any part of Europe that I'd ever seen. Leafs
growing from these trees were covered in little spots, like a ladybug. The
colors were unusual as well. Some leafs showed pastel spots while others were
black with angry red swirls. The fruit hanging from the branches was even more
bizarre. Red bulbs that appeared similar to pears in shape but were enormous hung from some branches. I found one that had fallen and stood it
up. I my estimation it weighted at least 50lbs and stood up as tall my belt
buckle. I removed my knife and sliced a portion off to try. However, what I
found upon cutting into it was that the fruit was actually a shell of some
sort. I broke a piece off to see what was contained within and

what I found
appeared to be hundreds of little grape sized berries. I was considering trying
one when suddenly I noticed the berries to begin to shuffle around a bit.
Something was inside this husk, hiding within. The shuffling grew more urgent, and I saw something begin to emerge. I did not wait around for it to introduce
itself. All I managed to see were its eyes. Terrible sight. They were
insectile, large and... some combination of red and brown. They looked both
agitated and apprehensive, anger fueled perhaps by confusion. A buzzing began
to emit from within the giant bulb, the sort of fury one hears when a wasp
buzzes too near their head. I became terrified and ran for my life. As sprinted
down the path that I'd once known so well, I passed under many of those fruit
bulbs, and sometimes I believed that I could hear rustling or buzzing from
within them.

After what felt like an eternity I finally emerged from the trees and back into the open. I looked around to see if I could identify where
I was, and that is when I noticed that path had been paved. Never had it been
more than just a dirt road, but now it looked... as impossible as it sounds, as
if it were paved in marble.

Then, but God's grace and love, I saw another person up ahead of me. I called out to him and he turned stood patiently. I began to
ramble on about the strange wildlife and vegetation that I'd found in the
woods, but he did not seem surprised.

He told me that I was lucky I'd not been bitten by one of them, as there was currently no cure. His accent was strange to me. I'd never heard it before in all of my travels. He spoke French, but every once in a while he'd throw in a word that I'd never heard of. I could tell by his speech that the word was supposed to be there though. I asked him about the marble road and he smiled as most proud natives of their land will when someone admires their landmarks and informed me that the road was nearing 500 years of use and still looked brand new. I asked him how this road could be so old when I'd never seen it. He asked me where I was from and I informed him that I born in southern France.

That's when the encounter grew stranger. He'd never heard of any place called France in his life. I laughed, thinking that he was making a game of me and asked him where exactly he thought he was currently standing in that case. He claimed we were in a country called Taured.

We spent a bit of that day walking together. He told me all about his so-called nation of Taured, and in return I told him of France. Apparently they shared the same location in the world as he knew of all the countries that Taured bordered, and all those nations border France as well. The language was also almost identical, but when he described certain aspects of day-to-day life in Taured, there were many differences. He told me how their economy was booming due to Taured's successful breeding of talking dogs. Nobles and aristocrats from all of Europe and Asia were flocking to his nation to purchase them or observe them in captivity. He told me that medical doctors from Taured's central college had mastered the science of reanimating primates from the dead with complete cognitive function. He informed me that human trials had begun already, but those that came back had no memories of who or what they were and would become violent easily. He invited me to accompany him to the capital city to see all of these marvels. I was mulling over the idea of going with him when suddenly I was alone once more. One moment my new friend was just chatting away about bringing back the dead, and in the next he was gone. I looked around for him and found that the marble road was gone as well. The hills and odd colored trees no longer decorated the landscape and even the air smelled a bit different.

I eventually came across some other travelers on a caravan and realized that I was right back on the original road heading across the French countryside in the direction of Spain. I asked some men in the caravan if they'd come across any strange trees or fruit, and they assured me they had not. Apparently they'd left the very same village I had earlier that day and encountered nothing out of the ordinary. When I got to Spain, I asked many of their leading geography experts, map makers and even some of their traveling diplomats if any of them had ever seen or heard of a

country, city,
town... anything called Taured. No one had. No one recalled seeing a marble road
or any of the landscapes that I'd described. Eventually I convinced myself that
it must have been a dream."

Larson nodded, "Thank you for sharing that. What Mr. Cornelius is describing is one of the most rare occurrences in nature, a Layer
Flux Anomaly. Even now we don't fully understand this phenomena enough to
advance past general theory. This country of Taured that he mentions has come
up a few times in the stranger end of history, usually as an unsolved mystery
or urban legend. A 21st Century story once circulated that a man passed through an airport with a questionable passport claiming to be from
Taured. He also indicated that it was in the general area of France. Top
researchers believe that it is a layer of reality that isn't in tune with ours.
If it were to merge at some point, we likely wouldn't even know it, as our
perception would simply adjust to accommodate its existence."

The old man Cornelius smiled knowingly before interjecting once more. "Oh, you'd notice it, although you wouldn't quite understand it.
Generally it shows up as something that seems wrong although all the tangible
data states otherwise."

Larson detected a certain tone of defiance in the old man
and was beginning to grow concerned as to what exactly he was hinting at.
Cornelius had been recruited for his brilliant mind and uncanny

abilities to adapt and comprehend new challenges, but he was also known to be arrogant and difficult when the mood struck.

“What are you suggesting Mr. Cornelius?”

“What I am suggesting Major Larson, is that perhaps all is not what it seems. Those strange feelings... or that sensation that something is wrong even though all physical evidence states otherwise… how often do you get them?”

“I suppose on occasion, but I hardly think there is some greater cause of this.”

“Are you sure? How about in cases of something that should be very well known to you? Your name for example; perhaps even the street that you grew up on or the name of your first goldfish. Over the last year I’ve felt this a lot. With all of this tampering and such, do you ever wonder why so many aspects of our lives feel alien to us?”

“Mr. Cornelius, that’s enough!” Copeland suddenly shouted.

“Now just wait a moment Dr. Copeland, I just want to ask one question,” the old man replied. “What was my name yesterday? I know that Cornelius isn’t right. If I think back I can picture my parents calling me Cornelius and everyone else I’ve ever known. I’ve signed this name countless times on legal documents. However, I know that it isn’t my name!”

“No! No more interrupting! We have a job to do here and...”

“They have the right to know!”

At that moment the lights in the room momentarily flickered. Larson rubbed his eyes, feeling the faintest itch somewhere behind them, like a
little tingle from his eyes to his brain. Then it passed.

“You were saying Major Larson?” a petite young lady of perhaps 19 years of age asked.

“You were just telling us that the governments of the world collected in Moscow Russia.”

The young woman was sitting at a computer desk that someone else, someone old and wise but perhaps a bit argumentative had occupied seconds
ago. At least that was what Larson
thought was going on. Sometimes that happened in this line of work.

“Yes, and as everyone here knows, from that gathering of world leaders came the groundwork for what we have now. The Axis Station, the
Board who over see what we do here, and of course, our core mission.”

“To Exist Until We Need Not Exist!” the excited researchers bellowed on cue.

“That’s correct, and thanks to the efforts of our very own Dr. Megan Copeland, we believe that this will be the final Recalculation. Of
course, I believe that it has to be. Should we fail on this... Wait...”

Larson turned to Copeland. “Yes Major?” she asked.

"Megan... I just called you Megan Copeland."

"Of course, that's my name."

"Yeah, I just... did you ever have a nickname... something with an "S?" I could have sworn I used to call you something like... Savannah, or Serra... any of this sound familiar?"

"No, I've always been Megan Copeland. Well, Dr. Megan Copeland if we're keeping it professional.

"Right, sorry. Anyway, back on track. Why we must succeed today!"

The researchers and operators were now leaning forward. The good part at last. Larson was the only known survivor of a T.U.B.

"It happened right here, right in this very room. You were all here with me. (As he said this, he looked over at the young woman who seemed to just not quite fit in. Had he felt that way about her before the lights flickered? He certainly didn't think so.) We'd been working on many of the same operations, but we tried too many times. We wore down the Continuity too much. Too many re-fires."

"If we're writing over history with every Recalculation though, why is the Continuity affected at all?" asked someone in the back of the room.

"We don't know exactly why it happens, but the most widely accepted theory is that nothing is ever erased, it's simply pushed down to some unseen layer of the equation. It still counts, and it still puts some

sort of
pressure on the intangible straps that hold existence together. If we
Recalculate too many times, I suppose we run out of room. It overloads
something that we don't fully comprehend."

According to the Laws of Physics, a T.U.B. shouldn't even be possible. Basic thermodynamics, the Law of Conservation of Energy, even the
concept of a Zero Energy Universe all insist that a T.U.B. can't happen. Yet,
they can. It's because all of those physical laws refer to energy or mass or
conversion and so on. Scientist have cracked all sorts of physical and temporal
mysteries over the last few eons or so, but the one that evades us all, the one
that trumps everything... is the nature of existence.
Everything must conform to this. Humans, animals, galaxies
and energy itself, from the largest super planet to the tiniest sub-particle,
each and every thing must exist. If the building blocks of existence collapse,
there is no law of physics in the book that will save you. That energy doesn't
just cease converting, it ceases being."

"Tell us about the T.U.B." Dr. Copeland demanded. Larson
took notice of how closely she was standing to him. He knew the woman well, had
been working with her for years, but the look in her eyes of hunger and
impatience made him a bit nervous.

"We started where we always do, at the only confirmable
point of stability. As most of you have probably heard, the history that we

think we know of the world, even that which was salvaged by the Society, is likely incorrect. Sadly we have almost no way of really knowing how much of it is wrong, and that is one of the reasons why we established this base so far away for Earth.

Have any of you ever wondered why we don’t cease to exist as soon as we apply a Recalculation? After all, we’re changing history. By that logic, as any Recalculation should potentially alter the timeline to a point where we likely wouldn’t remain in this present to observe it.”

“Because Recalculations don’t change anything until you apply the Realignment,” came an answer from the staff.

“That is partially correct. Recalculations do affect the Earth’s history as soon as they are applied. However, our station here exists on the Temporal Axis Theory. That’s why we have to perform all of these Recalculations from this very specific location in space. We are able to phase this station into a pocket of time that allows us to observe our changes without them changing us. But we cannot remain here forever, and once we feel that all of our repairs have fixed the issue, we must Realign ourselves, so to speak. Once that happens, well, our little motto will make a lot more sense. We will be reshuffled into the new history, and all of this will cease to be.

Now, to shed some light on how we know where to start with our Recalculations, allow me to introduce you to Eric, one of our most invaluable members.”

One of the scientist who was standing near the blackboard wheels out a table. Sitting atop the table is a jar full of murky liquid and a computer monitor. Cables run from somewhere behind the jar to the monitor. A single cursor prompt flashes on the screen.

"This is Eric. Or at least what is left of him. Within the jar is a sliver of Eric's brain. It's active. Eric lived before The Overload and was one of the first recruits pulled for this project once the Axis bases were established. During his time here he worked with a team much like all of you. He led them much as I do and he performed Recalculations in support of the same..."

DIFFERENT!

That word suddenly exploded in Larson's head. Eric's mission wasn't different though... was it? It's always been about preventing the Overload...

"Major, something wrong?" Copeland asked.

Ummm, no, sorry, where was I? Yes, Eric was also the man in charge who gave the tragic orders to initiate the first and only known Realignment."

A gasp of nervousness sounded from the crew.

"That's right. We have Realigned once before. I am confident that all of you can assume that since we are still here working that it did not repair our history. A lot of what I am telling you today is classified. The Board has granted me permission though to debrief you all completely. We do not want another T.U.B. and perhaps it was withholding this information last time that led to failure..."

"So, what you're telling us is that what we think and know to be Earth's history could be completely incorrect?" Dr. Copeland asked, although she was simply doing so to move along the lecture. She'd received the same instructions from the Board as Larson.

"Yes and no. Not all of it was changed the first time. Thanks to Eric we can establish somewhat of a baseline for a starting point. But because of the first attempted Realignment, we can no longer pinpoint for sure the Prime Catalyst. Eric was killed the first time around, but as most of you do know, the Board's chambers are protected. Even during Realignment they can retain awareness for a brief period, a few minutes at most, but long enough for them to take the appropriate steps. Eric was protected within the Board's chambers when it happened, and although he died, his brain was recovered in time to be preserved. An organic computer that cannot crash so long as it's fed the right impulse charges to keep it going."

The young woman who Larson couldn't quite comprehend raised her hand.
"Sir, can we see Eric function?"

"Certainly. If it weren't for Eric we likely wouldn't know where to even look to begin any sort of Recalculations. First off, let me ask you all a question. I want you to type the answer on your screen and send it to the main monitor behind me. I want to do a bit of comparison. Ready?"

The team nodded.

"What is the name of our planet?"

The clicking of many keyboards began, and one by one the answer appeared on the large screen mounted to the wall. The word Earth appeared 14 times on the screen with the corresponding console number for each staffer's computer.

"Very good, that is correct. Next question, which famous leader defeated Darius the 3rd of Persia at the Battle of Gaugamela?"

Once more answers began to appear on the screen. Alexander the Great was the unanimous choice.

"Nice work, I'd almost think I was working with the world's greatest historical minds here," Larson joked. The room lit up for a moment with light-hearted chuckles. Lawson wasn't known for his sense of humor, and it was always a pleasant surprise when he allowed a small bit of levity to escape.

He continued down the line.

"At what famous battle was Hannibal defeated?"

"Zama."

"Where was paper invented?"

"China."

"Where was the Chera Dynasty created?"

"India."

Larson looked around the room for a moment before asking the next question.
"What battle led to Macedonia becoming a Roman province?"

The questions rattled on, and slowly but surely, they began to grow strange. Caesar was suddenly regarded as a "President" instead of an
Emperor. Robert Fulton still invented the steamboat, but it was now called "The
Gateway" instead of The Clermont. Fossil fuels were not refined into a usable
source of energy on time, causing the advancement of automobiles to be delayed.

"Now that we have all of your answers, answers that we know came from a possibly tainted history, let's talk to Eric. His brain, thanks to
the protections of the Board's safety protocols, holds knowledge from before
the first Realignment. He knows the 'real' history, in other words."

"Caesar was an Emperor, Fulton's boat was called The Clermont, and the dates of fossil fuel refinement are different. See, we
believe that what Eric recalls is the real history of Earth, and what most of

you… myself as well really, understand to be the original run of history is in
fact a result of the first mission's failure."

"I don't like that…" a gentleman with a long mustache and thinning white hair exclaimed. "Just thinking about it makes my head hurt…
everything we know… everything we've been taught… all false…?"

"And that is our fault, this Department," Larson replied. "When we activated the first Realignment we altered history forever. The
original goal was to space out societal advancement in such a way that
the Big Press wouldn't cluster as it did. The Board believed that if we could
spread out the Communication Age by just a few hundred years then we could
prevent the Overload. No loss of information, no Dim Ages, no collapse of
society. The first attempted round of Recalculations appears to have been
focused around the time of the Roman Empire and beyond. What data we do have
suggests that Eric and his team were confident they'd gotten it right.
Confident enough to push the button to activate the Realignment, anyway; and
that is what we've been trying to repair for the last year."

"Sir… what you're saying cannot be right. If a Realignment to correct the Overload of 2102 were set into motion, how is it that any of us
know about the Overload? Shouldn't it have all been altered, for better or for
worse?"

In that moment the Major felt a wave of dizziness come over him. There it was, the golden question. The very question he'd never allowed himself to ponder. Larson always tried to convince himself that the Overload would have simply happened anyway. But that didn't sit right with him either. If Eric was trying to correct history to prevent the Big Press by moving dates around or changing early governments, how could it be that the exact same...

Then he remembered the dream, the one that had awoken him on this very morning with a racing heartbeat. In this dream he was running across a vast field. Something was chasing him, something enormous and dark; something that was older than the cosmos and wise beyond any comprehension. He continued to run and as he did, his mind's eye drifted upward, revealing that he was running on one giant circle, doomed to repeat his steps. He wasn't sure right now if his dream meant anything, he wasn't sure how he suddenly knew what he knew, but he felt compelled to follow his instincts.

"Because our Department caused it."

Once he said it, he felt better. He didn't like the look on his assistant's face though. She seemed to be silently fuming with rage. Why this would bother her so much he did not know.

"We don't know everything concerning Eric's first mission. He can only answer short, simple and direct questions, so it's impossible for

us to fully interrogate him. If we push him too far, we risk permanent damage
to the system that communicates with him. What we do know however is that
Eric's first mission had other, far more classified elements than just the Big
Press. They were working on something else, but we can't get that data from him
and the Board either refuses to debrief or was equally affected by the
Realignment and no longer know themselves. All I know for sure is that my
mission has always been to correct the timeline enough to prevent the Overload.
That's what I was working on last time anyway...

The last Recalculation that I ordered on that day caused the T.U.B.
I survived it only because the Board of Directors has a functioning kill switch. It can restart an event at a pre-programed point in
time. Once the point is set, it creates one Temporal Handshake between that
date and the present. I was in their chambers when I gave the last
Recalculation order. Honestly by that point I suspected that a T.U.B. was
possible, we'd been reshaping the time frame a lot, but I didn't suspect we were
that close. When it happened..."

"Wait just a minute," a middle aged woman wearing an olivedrab dress and slim bifocals said with agitation in her voice. "If this entire
mission is to repair the actions of Eric's Realignment, then what was Eric's
original purpose? Why were we altering time in the first place, what did we

do?"

The Major rubbed his eyes in annoyance. They were itching again. Probably all the smokers in the room... he was going to have to talk to the Board about banning cigarettes in the data room. He was about to tell them about the T.U.B. but he also felt as though he was about to explore some other... slightly more taboo discussion.

When he opened his eyes, he saw that a heavyset man in a brown suit was suddenly occupying a desk that seemed as though it should belong to someone else. He tried to picture who should be there, and it caused his head to swim in a dizzy sensation that wasn't quite unpleasant but was still quite undesirable.

"Major Larkson, we really do need to proceed," Dr. Copeland stated firmly. "Please tell us about the T.U.B."

"It's Larson..." he began to reply, but suddenly felt a bit silly. He started the sentence with conviction and a bit of annoyance that his long time colleague and friend would mispronounce his name. By the time he said the name 'Larson' out loud though, it felt fictitious, like a child giving a false name when they're caught shoplifting candy from a store. It lingered though. The third instance in the last hour where he felt his eyes itch and suddenly couldn't comprehend something that should be as relatable to himself as his parent's first names or the city he grew up in.

"Sorry doctor, I was just thinking out loud again. The T.U.B.... yeah... I had inputted the Recalculation as normal and waited for my tablet to display the results. However, the tablet suddenly goes black. With no warning or real explanation the members of the Board calmly stand up. They all produce their little tablets from their pockets, just as nonchalantly as someone removes their wallet to pay at a restaurant. They start tapping away and that's when I see it rise from the center of their table.

The kill switch; I'd never seen the thing before; honestly I wasn't even sure if I believed it existed. But when I saw it when I saw the looks on their faces, I knew what I was looking at. They didn't appear afraid or even concerned; they just looked a little annoyed. They knew they'd have to start again.

'Enjoy the show,' one of them says to me. They don't have names and I have no clue which one it was, but there was certainly malice in the tone. I suppose forcing me to watch the collapse of time, space and matter qualifies as a punishment.

The T.U.B. starts. I gazed out of the giant glass wall in the Board's main conference room and watched as the entire universe around me begins to fade out. It doesn't just happen in a sudden blink. It takes a few minutes, and I felt every bit of it. Stars, galaxies, the solar system and everything else simply dimmed, like using a dimmer switch on a light bulb. As

this happened though, I dimmed as well. Everything that ever was or ever could
be is literally vanishing in front of my eyes.
This means that everything that made me, every breath I took from the time I was born, everything I ever tasted, touched, learned, loved,
feared or knew… it was all fading away. I'll never forget what it felt like to
experience my entire identity melt away all at once. I forgot who I was, what I
was, where I was. I became nothing, and to be buried underneath the weight of
all that nothing…
It felt like an eternity. I was in the darkness, I couldn't
move, couldn't think. I was reduced to something below an ameba because at
least an ameba has a designed purpose. For what could have been mere seconds or
perhaps even centuries I existed in some form that I will never comprehend. We
learn through exposure, and within that place that isn't a place at all, that
is nothing, I failed to exist. The darkness gave me nothing to grasp onto. I
couldn't experience emotions because no such thing existed.
All I know is that at some point the kill switch must have
finally completed its task because I was standing before the Board receiving
my instructions to begin this project. They tell me that we cannot go home
until the timeline is repaired once and for all."

"Then let's do it," Dr. Copeland whispered and handed Larkson the tablet.

He walked over to the blackboard and began to input information. The scientists stood back, smiling and anxious. After carefully

verifying his input into the tablet, the Major stepped back. His eyes seemed
distant, a stoic leader in deep thought. Then, seemingly struck with
inspiration, Larkson removed a folded piece of paper from the pocket of his
jacket. His team looked on in wonder.

“Some last minute notes Major?” Copeland asked.

“Yes,” he answered, and suddenly began to input more instructions and calculations into the tablet. As he did, he quickly backed
away from Copeland, creating enough space to prevent any sudden grab at the
device in his hand.

“What are you doing Larkson? The device was set to our precise measurements. Why are you changing things?”

A man stood from behind a computer and quickly pointed to the large monitor on the wall.
“I just synced our computers to the tablet, look what he’s doing!” he shouted in panic.

All eyes shot to the large monitor on the wall. What they saw on the monitor is what Larkson saw on the tablet, what he’d programmed into
the tablet. The screen was red with a brief warning displayed above two digital
buttons. One read ‘CANCEL’ the other read ‘INITIATE.’

It wasn’t the buttons or the red screen that now had the room in a panic, but rather the warning printed above.

DANGER: YOU HAVE UNLOCKED THE MASTER RESET COMMAND. IF THIS

SCREEN HAS BEEN REACHED IN ERROR, PLEASE PRESS CANCEL IMMEDIATELY AND REPORT
THIS INCIDENT TO THE BOARD. PRESSING INITIATE WILL UNDO ALL RECALCULATIONS MADE
FROM THE BEGINNING OF THIS OPERATION. THE SPECIFIC TIMELINE OF ORIGIN WILL
RESTORE. ALL CHANGES WILL BE LOST. RESETING AT THIS LEVEL CARRIES THE POTENTIAL
FOR COMPLETE AND TOTAL UNIVERSAL REALLIGNMENT. THE TEMPORAL BARRIER THAT
SHIELDS YOUR AXIS POINT WILL BE INEFFECTIVE IN PREVENTING AXIS CREW FROM
EXPERIENCING CAUSE AND EFFECT. BOARD MEMBER KILL SWITCH AND TEMPORAL HANDSHAKE
PROTOCAL WILL BE INEFFECTIVE IN PREVENTING BOARD MEMBERS FROM EXPERIENCING
CAUSE AND EFFECT.

“Major! Explain this please! How did you activate that screen? What are you planning?” Copeland asked in a stern, flat tone.

“I figured we had to try something new,” he answered, and handed her the piece of paper. She read its content:

To the crew of Joint Base Tara,

Greetings. My name is Admiral James Carr. I am the acting Post Commander for the 87th Sector, Axis 2. I am contacting you from
the 34th Millennium with grave news. Should you receive this notice
it means that my Recalculations were successful. This is likely the last
opportunity I will have to Recalculate before we cause a T.U.B. Be advised, the
measurements that you believe are correct will fail. This failure will initiate

another T.U.B. Your Board members will attempt to activate their kill switch
and reset the event. However, what the Board has failed to inform you of is
that your operation has failed thousands times. You no doubt believe this is
your second time arriving at the final Recalculation of this mission. That is
false. By our estimations this is your 9316th attempt. Each and every time a T.U.B. has occurred. This time your Board will cause a T.U.B. of
their own when they attempt the Handshake. They have written over these events
too many times, and even though your base is shielded from the majority of the
impact caused by damaging the Continuity fibers, everything, even the Board,
has a limit. Your only hope now is to initiate a complete reset and allow
history to replay. I am Recalculating to modify your tablet to include a reset
option that was never available to anyone besides the highest level of the
Board.
Major Larkson, be advised that your Board is Recalculating within your Axis Station. Those strange sensations that you've been
experiencing today are a direct result of these activities. However, this
notification is unique to today. You must break the cycle now though as there
will be no further opportunities.
I am the last human in existence. I have tried to repair the universe by Recalculating your actions. However, I have run out of time just as
you have. If you fail, I fail.

Godspeed Joint Base Tara

"So that's it?" Copeland demanded with rage and terror in her eyes. "You find this note in your pocket and decide to just erase the
entire history of the Earth? Are you really going to void all of humanity because
of some nonsense scribbled on a piece of paper?"

"Flip the paper over," Larkson replied.

Copeland did as he instructed. Six words were printed on the back of the note:

Don't trust Copeland. You are Eric.

"Who are you?" the Major demanded.

"Daniel, I am Megan Copeland. We've been working together for a year. You know me very well."

"Your name isn't Megan... I know it isn't. When we left the Board today, I called you something else. Why is your name Megan now?"

"Daniel, you need to calm down and hand me the tablet."

"What was Eric's mission? If all of this, the Axis, the Board... if all of this is to correct the Overload, then why the hell does
everyone here even know about the Overload post Realignment? I want you to tell
me what the hell Eric... what the hell I was doing when we Realigned!"

"Daniel, you have to relax and give me the..."

"Shut the fuck up! Ask Eric, ask him what his original mission was!"

"No."

Larkson slid his thumb to the "Initiate" button. Copeland realized that should he apply the slightest amount of contact he could likely
set off the event.

"ASK HIM!! ASK HIM NOW! He screamed at her.

"Does it really matter Daniel?" she whispered.

"I want to know!" shouted one of the team members.

"Me too," called out another. "I want to know why I've been inputting this data for a year. I want to know why I always feel like half of
my memories are wrong."

"We all do!" announced one of the scientists who'd been manning the blackboard.

Without waiting for Copeland's reply, he began to input the question into the device that communicated with the undying brain trapped within
the jar.

The response appeared at once. A single word on a screen accompanied by shocked gasps from those in attendance; all except for Dr.
Copeland, who simply looked as though she were a cheating spouse who'd just
been caught by a faithful husband.

"We... we never thought..." she began.

Larkson pressed the Initiate button.

Better luck next time.

Lightning Source UK Ltd.
Milton Keynes UK
UKHW011821160819
348101UK00001B/66/P

9 781793 085825